Five Nights at

TALES FROM THE PIZZAPLEX

#7 TIGER ROCK

Five Nights at Freddy's™

TALES FROM THE PIZZAPLEX

#7 TIGER ROCK

BY

SCOTT CAWTHON
KELLY PARRA
ANDREA WAGGENER

Scholastic Inc.

Photo of TV static: © Klikk/Dreamstime

All rights reserved. Published by Scholastic Inc., *Publishers since 1920*. SCHOLASTIC and associated logos are trademarks and/or registered trademarks of Scholastic Inc.

The publisher does not have any control over and does not assume any responsibility for author or third-party websites or their content.

This book is a work of fiction. Names, characters, places, and incidents are either the product of the author's imagination or are used fictitiously, and any resemblance to actual persons, living or dead, business establishments, events, or locales is entirely coincidental.

Library of Congress Cataloging-in-Publication Data available

ISBN 978-1-338-87135-7

10 9 8 7 6 5 4 3 2 1   23 24 25 26 27

Printed in the U.S.A.   131

First printing 2023 • Book design by Jeff Shake

TABLE OF CONTENTS

TIGER ROCK

H EY!" KAI PROTESTED, "ARE YOU TRYING TO PULL MY ARM OFF?"

Stepping through the grand quadruple-door glass and gleaming chrome entrance to the Freddy Fazbear Mega Pizzaplex, Kai inhaled the aromas of spicy pizza sauce and sweet cotton candy as he shook off his over-eager, amped-up friend. Todd, as usual, didn't think Kai was moving fast enough.

Asher, the last of the "Timeless Trio," as Kai and his two best buddies called themselves, laughed as he followed Kai and Todd inside. "Face it," Asher said, "you're just too slow, Kai."

Kai laughed, too. It was an old joke. Kai had been born on Oahu, and he'd spent his first seven years on the island with his native Hawaiian mother and his "cowboy" dad (born and raised on a ranch in Wyoming). Between the "Hawaiian Time" attitude of his mom and the "What's your hurry, pawdna?" mindset of his dad, Kai was known for being "chill." Todd regularly accused Kai of being so laid-back that he was practically horizontal.

"Come on, you guys!" Todd urged. He waved his

arms around and barely missed whacking a pretty teen girl in the face.

She shot Todd a dirty look. He was oblivious to it, as usual—too busy looking around.

Kai couldn't blame him. The Pizzaplex was seriously cool, maybe the only fun place in their small town.

They'd been thrilled when it was built, but it was no longer new to Kai, Todd, and Asher. They'd seen the blacklight play area for the little kids—climbing toys, slides, and foam building blocks set up around a glitter-ball pit. They'd gazed up at the stained-glass cupola that capped the center of the Pizzaplex's dome, and they'd been inside the castle-like two-story theater rotunda that sat under the kaleidoscopic spray of light that came through the stained glass. They'd investigated every single one of the game venues and shops and restaurants. They'd eaten at least a dozen pizzas in the flashy neon-lit, mirrored-ceilinged main dining room, and they'd bought more than their fair share of Freddy's-themed clothing and souvenirs. They'd driven the go-carts on the tracks that crisscrossed over and under the walkways connected to all the various parts of the Pizzaplex, and they'd ridden, several times, the roller coaster that swooped throughout the Pizzaplex, its tracks entwining with a seemingly endless maze of colorful climbing tubes. They'd watched the animatronic performances, and they knew by heart all the rock and pop songs the animatronics played and all the themed music pounding from the various game areas. They also knew the sounds of the games—the pings and beeps, the buzzes and vrooms, the hums and dings.

By now, Kai and his friends knew the bedazzled chaos of the Pizzaplex as well as they knew one another's homes. In fact, before Kai went to sleep at night, he often closed his eyes and lost himself in the endlessly constant motion of the Pizzaplex's brilliant lights, cheery music, and buoyant crowds. The otherworldly, over-the-top magnificence of the Pizzaplex cloaked the everyday-life stuff that sometimes got him down.

But despite this familiarity, Todd was always wide-eyed, almost starstruck, when they were here. He acted as if each of their visits to the magical fun dome was their first. But that was Todd. He was all about "being present."

"You have to make every moment count," Todd liked to say.

Todd had been the first to call them the Timeless Trio, a name he'd picked because they didn't fit in with the rest of their sixth-grade class. "Time is a construct. It doesn't exist. The only real thing is now," he'd declared. Kai and Asher didn't really get Todd's endless babblings about the "illusory nature of time," but they thought the name was cool.

"Come on," Todd repeated for at least the third time.

He tried to grab Kai's arm again. Kai sidestepped his friend and shook his head. He wondered, not for the first time, why someone who lived in the present was always in such a hurry.

"The Storyteller's Tree isn't going anywhere," Kai said.

As Kai followed Todd through the boisterous Pizzaplex crowd, he had to admit that he, too, was excited about seeing the tree. They hadn't been to the Pizzaplex in a couple weeks, and in that time, they'd overheard several kids at school talking about the tree that housed The Storyteller, a cutting-edge program that was supposed to feed story lines to the entertaining animatronics.

"Can you imagine the code that went into programming The Storyteller?" Asher had asked after they'd heard about it. Asher had gone online to read up on the new Pizzaplex feature, and he'd talked endlessly about it, using programming jargon that neither Kai nor Todd understood.

Even though Kai, Todd, and Asher were close friends, they couldn't have been more different. Kai, who knew his name meant "sea," was pretty relaxed about life in general. Yeah, things sometimes got to him, but most of the time, he could "go with the flow," something his mom always encouraged him to do. That was her nature. Kai's mom was an ER nurse but somehow, she never let the stress get to her. She didn't get rattled, no matter how many long hours she had to work or what she had to deal with.

"You have to ride the waves of life, Kai," she often told him.

In Hawaii, his mom had literally ridden the waves.

She'd just started teaching Kai to surf when his dad had moved to the mainland to run a start-up real estate development company, and they'd moved here, to a town a thousand miles from the nearest waves. Kai missed the ocean, but he was okay with where they lived now. He liked how the place had seasons, how the tree leaves turned orange and yellow in the fall and how snow fell in the winter. It was an okay trade-off for ocean waves.

Kai hadn't left the island behind him, though. Looking more like his black-haired, brown-eyed, and dark-skinned mom than his blond, blue-eyed dad (his sister was the opposite—she and Kai barely looked related), Kai also had his mother's short, slight shape. This squat appearance combined with the Hawaiian shirts and baggy cotton pants he preferred to the solid-color T-shirts and jeans of his classmates made him stand out. So did his tendency to zone out and daydream. Because Kai's mind wandered so much, he didn't do so well in school. He didn't care much about what he was being taught. He was more interested in nature and art and the spirit world.

In contrast to Kai, Todd was tall, skinny, and frenetic. With long, usually messy hair nearly as orange as the average carrot and a pale face painted almost brown by freckles, Todd stood out in school as much, or more, than Kai did. Todd, however, had no trouble with his schoolwork. He was a straight-A student who loved to learn. When he wasn't hanging out with Kai and Asher, Todd was always sprawled on his bed reading a book, his foot jittering the whole time. His room was so stuffed with books that there was barely enough room for his furniture—or for Asher and Kai when they visited him.

And then there was Asher. If he hadn't been a total tech geek, Asher might have fit in at school. With brown hair and eyes and a height that was average for an eleven-year-old, he looked pretty normal. Kai had even over-heard some girls talking about how cute Asher was. "Too bad he's so weird," one of the girls had said.

And yeah, Asher was a little weird. He was totally obsessed with computers and robotics and science fiction, so much so that he and his little brother, Alex, who could have been a slightly younger Asher clone, often spoke to each other in binary code. More than once, Kai had heard Alex say to Asher, "01100100 01101111 01101111 01100110 01110101 01110011." Asher told Kai that it meant "doofus."

"Wouldn't it be faster to just say 'doofus'?" Kai had asked.

"Sure," Asher had said. "But Alex and I get in trouble when we call each other names."

Asher's parents hadn't learned binary.

"Oh man!" Todd cried out.

Kai blinked and realized that while his mind had been wandering, they'd reached the center of the Pizzaplex. They were standing in front of The Storyteller's Tree.

And it was enveloped in plastic, with a rope barrier around its base.

"What happened?" Asher asked aloud to no one in particular.

A middle-aged man wearing the Pizzaplex "uniform" of a red shirt and black pants looked up from sweep-ing confetti near the bulging fiber-optic "roots" of the tree. "There was some kind of glitch," the man said. He rubbed the rough stubble on his square chin and shook his head. "It's only been up three weeks, and I hear they're going to take it down."

"What? Already?" Asher frowned up at the tree.

Kai followed the direction of Asher's gaze. What he saw gave him the willies, and he wasn't sure why. Maybe it was because the clear plastic wrapped around the tree's bloated, mottled-yellow trunk and its outstretched rainbow-colored limbs made the tree look like some kind of robed, phantom monster. Kai could easily picture the gigantic tree suddenly uprooting itself to stomp through the Pizzaplex. In Kai's mind, the tree reached out with its long skeletal branches to pluck children from the—

"Kai!" Todd was tugging on his arm again.

". . . picked a baobab tree because those trees have such big trunks," Asher was saying. "I think it was a great choice because the trees are the stuff of legend."

"A redwood tree would have been better," Todd said.

"No way," Asher said. "A redwood would have been too tall."

"Well, it wouldn't have been a real redwood," Todd said. "But redwoods have big trunks, too, and at least they're American trees."

"Why does it have to be American?" Asher asked. "Your shoes are made in China."

"So what? My shoes aren't a tree," Todd said.

Kai shook his head. He'd learned that the best thing to do when Todd and Asher fought was to just let them bicker. Todd and Asher had been friends since they were old enough to talk, and that was just the way they were with each other.

Asher turned away from Todd, ending the debate. He

pressed up against the rope barrier that had been strung around the tree's base. "I wish I could see in there," Asher said. "I wonder what went wrong with the program. I thought the basis of the program's algorithm was sound, and the idea of having one program generate all the stories for the animatronic characters was off-the-charts genius. Why pay a bunch of writers when you could just build one story-creation program?"

Todd snorted. "No way. A computer program can't take the place of a writer. There's no way a program could be advanced enough to replace people's imaginations."

Asher shook his head. "Mark Twain said it a long time ago: 'There's no such thing as a new idea.' Humans may like thinking their imaginations are all that, but really, nothing's original anymore. It's all just retelling old stories in a slightly different way. That's why having a computer program do it is so brill."

"Well, it must not have been *that* brill," Todd said, "if they shut it down so fast."

Todd reached for a cuff of Asher's long-sleeved orange-and-blue-plaid flannel shirt. The flannel shirt was another one of the things that set Asher apart: he always wore bright plaid flannel shirts, year-round—he even had summer flannel shirts with cut-off sleeves. It was different, but it was Asher.

"Come on, Ash," Todd said. "It's closed. Let's go do something else."

Asher sighed dramatically. He let Todd drag him away from The Storyteller's Tree.

"I want to check out the VR booth," Kai said.

"You would," Asher said. But he gave Kai one of his lopsided grins.

"I'm up for that," Todd said. He bounced on the balls of his feet. "Let's go for it."

The Pizzaplex, laid out like a big pizza, was easy to navigate. You just had to remember the order of the venues and where they landed on the edges of the "pie." The VR booth, Kai knew, was on the far side of The Storyteller's Tree. Because the tree, the big theater, and the kids' play area filled the center of the Pizzaplex, Kai and his friends would have to go around half the pizza to get to the VR booth.

"Wanna get a pizza on the way?" Todd asked as he started trotting away from The Storyteller's Tree, motioning for Asher and Kai to keep up with him.

"We just ate breakfast," Asher said as he jogged to catch up to Todd.

"There's always room for pizza," Todd singsonged, glancing over his shoulder.

"Not at ten in the morning," Asher said. "And slow down. The VR booth isn't going anywhere."

"That's what Kai said about The Storyteller's Tree," Todd said. But he reduced his speed to a fast walk.

"That tree looks like something you'd see in a strange dream," Kai said. Glancing to his right, he looked up at a purple branch that stretched out over them as they passed the Role Play area.

"Yeah," Todd agreed. "Or like something you'd see in a fantasy flick. They'd have trees like that in a place called Rainbow World."

Kai laughed. "Yeah. And little multicolored creatures living in the branches."

"Hey, right," Todd said, getting into it. "And they eat rainbow-colored food. Green pizza and yellow cookies."

"Ew," Asher said. He made a face. "Green pizza?"

Todd twisted his mouth. "Okay, maybe not green pizza. That's like the moss that grows on the big tree in my backyard. Yuck. I had a dream the other night that moss was growing really fast all over my room. It was trying to grow on me and eat me."

Todd stopped walking so abruptly that Asher ran into him. A young mom holding hands with two toddlers had to stutter-step to avoid the Todd–Asher collision. One of the toddlers dropped a sippy cup and let out a wail. As she retrieved the plastic cup, the mom gave Todd a dirty look. He didn't notice.

Todd looked at Kai. "I read that dream interpretation book your mom recommended. Apparently, my dream means there's something I'm afraid of that I'm not facing. If I don't get ahold of my fears, they'll eat me alive." Todd shrugged and rolled his eyes. "Like, duh. I don't need a dream to tell me I'm afraid of pretty much everything."

"Yeah, well, you do okay for a scaredy-cat," Asher said, giving Todd a playful light slap to the back of his head.

Todd grinned and started walking again, as quickly as before. Asher fell in step beside him.

Kai forced his short legs to move fast enough to stay with his friends. "I've been working on lucid dreaming," Kai said as he walked. "You know, being aware that you're dreaming when you're dreaming. I've been playing around with it. And I've trained myself to wake up just by saying to myself, in the dream, 'Wake myself.' I just have to say it a couple times, and I can get myself out of any dream, like that." He snapped his fingers. "You could try it, Todd, if you have a scary dream."

Todd and Asher exchanged a glance. They both grinned, and Todd slowed so he could punch Kai in the arm. "You're weird."

Kai shrugged. He knew Asher and Todd didn't get his interest in the spirit world. Whatever.

"Hey, look!" Todd pointed. "The AR booth has a special thing today."

Kai looked up, past the heads of the kids and adults scattered in front of them. He saw an LED marquis that read, TODAY ONLY! SEE THE PIZZAPLEX TEN YEARS FROM NOW! TAKE A PEEK INTO THE FUTURE!

"That sounds fun," Kai said. "You guys mind if I go first?"

Asher shook his head. Todd said, "Go for it."

Kai and his friends reached the line for the AR booth. He was glad to see it wasn't busy yet. Only two girls were in line. They stood near the VR booth attendant, a twentysomething, long-haired guy who was sitting on a stool, looking like he was bored out of his mind. Both girls, who looked to be maybe thirteen or fourteen, were dark-haired. When they turned to look at Kai, Todd, and Asher, Kai decided they must be sisters. Even though they didn't look exactly alike, they both had unusually big green eyes.

"Hey," the tallest of the two girls said. She smiled.

"Hi," Todd said. "Have you done the VR before?"

For a guy who claimed to be afraid of everything, Kai thought, *Todd was astoundingly outgoing.* He'd talk to anyone.

"Twice," the girl said. "And I've had enough. My sister wants to see the future, though."

The second girl grinned. "I'm just curious."

"Him, too," Todd said, jabbing a thumb toward Kai.

Todd and the girls started chatting about the future and what it might be like in general. Kai zoned out and gazed past them at the Virtual Reality booth.

The AR unit reminded Kai of the glass-domed display case that held his mom's terrarium of Hawaiian plants— *a little bit of home*, she called it. His mom's terrarium had a wooden base, but the AR base was bright red. And instead of encasing plants, the AR unit's glass dome held one large gold chair that looked like a plush gilded throne. The AR user sat in the chair (a boy Kai recognized as being a year ahead of him at school was in the chair now) and wore a netlike headband that was covered with a woven mass of sensory nodes. The headband was what made the Pizzaplex's AR so awesome—it worked with the user's own senses so that the AR experience felt totally real in every way.

Kai couldn't wait to find out what he'd see when he used the VR headband to get a glimpse of the Pizzaplex's future. If Todd and Asher didn't mind waiting, he decided, he'd go for the ten-minute session so he could really get into it.

Kai's eyes widened as he looked out at an even brighter and shinier version of the Pizzaplex than he was used to. Sleeker, flashier, and noisier, this Pizzaplex was even higher tech than the current one.

It was also packed with hundreds of adults and kids dressed in mind-blowing clothes. The future Pizzaplex's patrons were wearing screaming hot colors at least three times brighter than any Kai had seen before. The colors were so electric that they almost looked alive.

The fabric appeared to be rippling in constant motion, but as Kai studied it, he realized it was an optical illusion caused by ebbing and flowing lights in the fabrics' weave. These seemingly-in-motion clothes looked like they were whipping around everyone who moved through the Pizzaplex. Pants appeared to rise up and down along legs like constantly climbing escalators. Shirts and blouses looked like they were billowing and quivering, rotating around the torsos of the women and girls and juddering up and down on the backs and chests of the men and boys. It was an incredible visual effect. Kai wondered how they got the thread in the fabric to do that; it reminded him of a bookmark he had that looked like a dolphin when you turned it one way and an orca when you turned it another way. Asher said the bookmark was made with something called lenticular printing. It was a technology that produced 3D images that could change depending on the angle they were seen from. The fabrics in this future world's clothes must have used something similar. The clothes were unbelievable!

Kai had a hard time believing that clothes would change that much in ten years. From what he'd seen in his parents' photo albums, the clothes they'd worn when they were Kai's age weren't that much different than what he wore now.

But whatever. This was VR. Kai would just go with it.

Kai watched a bullet-train-shaped roller coaster speed past overhead. The roller coaster whipped through the air like a serpent racing after prey. Its movement was a blur, and it looked totally magical because the roller coaster wasn't on tracks! It was literally flying.

"Wow!" Kai breathed, tilting his head back to see the

silver, comet-like coaster skim past overhead. His hair tickled his ears as the coaster stirred the air around him. The coaster's high-pitched drone reverberated through his ears.

Someone jostled Kai, and he grinned at the extraordinary realism of the VR experience. He pulled his attention from the roller coaster, and he blinked in surprise. He was looking up into the astonishingly real-looking eyes of a future version of Glamrock Freddy.

"Hello there," Freddy said.

"Uh, hi," Kai said. He goggled at the tan bear standing in front of him.

This is too much, he thought.

Whereas the animatronic performers in the present-day Pizzaplex were made of smooth metal, all their costumes and features painted on, this animatronic—though still metallic—looked more like a real bear, or sort of a real bear. Glamrock Freddy still had the wide face, protruding round ears, huge eyes, and massive toothy smile of the metal Freddy, so he didn't look like any bear you'd find in nature. But his fur and his features— his mouth, nose, and eyes—were sculpted of metal in such detail that they looked like real fur and real eyeballs and stuff. Over the real-bear metal fur, Glamrock Freddy wore his usual costume, but this costume wasn't painted on. Instead of a metal, black top hat welded to his metal head, Freddy's hat appeared to be made of real black felt. He also wore an actual fabric shirt with a light blue lightning bolt emblem, leather shoulder pads, and leather leggings. Real metal-studded black leather bands were around his wrists, and his claws were painted blue to match the lightning bolt. Like the clothing on the

Pizzaplex's visitors, Freddy's shirt appeared to jitter over his chest and back, and his leggings looked like they were sliding up and down in constant motion.

Kai nearly jumped out of his skin when this eye-popping Freddy stuck out a metallic furry-looking paw. "I'm Freddy," the future Freddy said in a deep, rumbly voice.

Kai hesitated, then raised his own plump, short-fingered hand. ."Kai," he said.

"Kai. That is a great name," Freddy said. Freddy dropped Kai's hand and put a metallic paw on Kai's shoulder. "How about I show you around? We have a lot of things to see in the Pizzaplex!"

"Uh, sure," Kai said.

For the next dizzying couple of minutes, Kai let Freddy lead him, paw on shoulder, along the walkway that circled the future Pizzaplex theater. The new theater resembled a castle like the old one, but it was made of what looked to be cut crystal and shimmering light. The theater's roof, like the one in the present-day Pizzaplex, stretched to the top of the Pizzaplex's domed roof. But this domed roof was different than the one he was used to. Instead of being made of stained glass, it was clear. The roof was so clear that Kai wasn't sure there was a roof at all. When Freddy noticed Kai's upward gaze, Freddy said, "A state-of-the-art force field protects the Pizzaplex while providing access to fresh air and a view of the pretty blue sky."

"Cool," Kai said as he watched a crow swoop overhead and perch in midair. The bird must have been resting on the force field.

"It doesn't zap anything, huh?" Kai said, pointing at the crow.

Freddy laughed a deep, growly laugh. "No zapping!"

Freddy continued on. He pointed out all the familiar entertainment venues—each of which had been obviously updated in flashy new ways.

The dining room, for instance, no longer had square tables. All the tables were of different, round-edged shapes, like amoebas, and they hovered legless in the air. The servers hovered, gliding a few inches off the ground in chunky red boots.

The cars in Roxy's Raceway had lost their tires; they skimmed along the crystal track like the way Kai had seen, in movies, airboats graze along the surface of the water in swamps. The cars had been completely made over and streamlined; they appeared almost like domed tubes.

Passing Bonnie Bowl, Kai watched balls that looked like spinning supernovas rocket along lanes so bright he had to squint. He peered into the laser tag area to see kids holding small cell phone–looking contraptions that fired phosphorescent streams of light.

As Glamrock Freddy and Kai made their way through the future Pizzaplex, Kai watched several animatronics interacting with kids. Although a sign outside the theater held a schedule of shows, the animatronics appeared to spend more time hanging out with the crowd than performing onstage. Kai overheard several snatches of conversations between the characters and the kids as he and Freddy toured the Pizzaplex. The animatronics' interaction was basic and a little stilted, kind of like how Freddy was talking to Kai with no contractions and speaking a little too flat to be normal, but it was cool that they were chatting.

"Here are our newest additions to the fun," Freddy said. He led Kai past an African Safari ride that looked super realistic, scarily so, and a log flume ride that had rocket-like contraptions jetting through churning waves. Then he continued on toward an area labeled TIGER ROCK TRAMPOLINE.

"Oh, look," Freddy said as they approached an enormous space filled with dozens of delighted kids bouncing around and doing somersaults. They leaped through the air that warped a bit—the way the sky rippled over a paved road on a hot day.

"It is Tiger Rock himself," Freddy said. "Hello, Tiger Rock. Come meet Kai. He is our newest visitor."

Kai raised an eyebrow when he saw a huge, flowing white robe covered in sparkly sequins and crystal beads that had the same motion-like quality of the other clothes Kai had seen in this future Pizzaplex. The robe swirled, and what was in the robe turned to face Kai.

Kai, blinking in awe, found himself looking up into the gaze of a metallic white tiger. The tiger, whose white fur was as realistically hairlike as Freddy's, wore white leather bell-bottomed pants studded with gold baubles; the baubles looked like they were dancing and twirling. A gold medallion hung around the tiger's neck.

"Hey, there, Kai," Tiger Rock said. "Tiger Rock at your service."

"You will be in good hands with Tiger Rock," Freddy said. "It was nice to meet you, Kai."

"Uh, you too, Freddy," Kai said. "Thanks for the tour."

Freddy took off his top hat and tipped it toward Kai, who lifted a hand to wave good-bye. Then he looked back at Tiger Rock.

Tiger Rock leaned forward and studied Kai with far more interest than Freddy had shown. More interest, in fact, than anyone had ever shown in Kai. Tiger Rock's gaze was almost searing as Tiger Rock examined Kai from head to toe. Finally, Tiger Rock reached out and took Kai's hand. He raised it so quickly and shook it so emphatically that the pull and jerk motion actually hurt Kai's shoulder.

Tiger Rock pumped Kai's hand up and down several times, much longer than was normal for a handshake. Kai finally snatched his hand back. With his other hand, he casually rubbed his shoulder.

Tiger Rock flashed a wide mouthful of teeth at Kai. "It's super great to meet you, Kai. Aloha ʻauinalā."

Kai nodded, surprised by the animatronic tiger's knowledge. "Hello to you, too! You speak Hawaiian?"

Tiger Rock winked. "I know a lot of things."

"That's impressive," Kai said. "Even my friends don't know any Hawaiian."

"Oh, I love learning," Tiger Rock said. "I'll learn anything I can." He leaned down and cocked his head. "It's all in how you pay attention and take in what you see and hear. You feel me?"

Kai chuckled. Unlike Freddy and the other animatronics Kai had overheard, Tiger Rock had some flair. Not only was he more fluid, speaking more naturally with contractions, he also spoke with a little bit of swag, like a DJ on the radio. Kai liked Tiger Rock.

"How would you like to learn something?" Tiger Rock asked Kai.

"Like what?"

Tiger Rock leaned down and lowered his voice to an "I've got a secret" whisper. "I can show you how things work around here," Tiger Rock said, cocking his head and studying Kai like he was the most fascinating boy in the world.

Kai kind of liked the attention. He studied Tiger Rock right back.

Tiger Rock had the normal broad, round face of a tiger, with circular ears jutting from the top of his head. The shape of his head and face, however, was where Tiger Rock's normalcy stopped. Whereas most white tigers—at least ones in the pictures Kai had seen—had strong black stripes encircling a dark muzzle, Tiger Rock's face was predominately white. The few black stripes Tiger Rock had were faint, and they radiated out from his muzzle to form a diamond pattern that embraced his white nose and mouth. Instead of the usual spray of white tiger whiskers, Tiger Rock had just a few almost incandescent whiskers. And instead of a normal tiger's white teeth, Tiger Rock had nearly transparent teeth that appeared to pulse with softly colored light. Tiger Rock's most striking feature, though, was his eyes. The white tigers Kai had seen in pictures had pale blue eyes, but there was nothing pale about Tiger Rock's eyes. His eyes were lit up like the most dazzling neon and were two different colors as well. One eye was deep emerald green, and the other was bright blue.

"Sure," Kai said when he realized he'd been staring. "I'd like that."

"Right on!" Tiger Rock said.

Tiger Rock wrapped a humongous paw around Kai's left arm. The animatronic tiger squeezed his metal paw pads around Kai's yellow and purple Hawaiian shirt sleeve. The pressure was steady but not uncomfortable.

"Let's go!" Tiger Rock said.

Kai grinned. This was the best VR experience he'd ever had.

Kai found himself in a part of the Pizzaplex he'd never seen before. Tiger Rock, still with a grip on Kai's arm, was leading Kai along a glistening white-walled corridor lined with a futuristic conveyor belt. All manner of robots—large and small, human- or animal-shaped, and boxy, utilitarian-shaped—rode the belt.

"These are the helper bots," Tiger Rock said. He removed his paw from Kai's arm and waved at a triangular-shaped robot carrying a tool that looked like a fancy broom. "Hey, Henry," Tiger Rock said.

The robot with the broom lifted a spatula-shaped appendage. He made a funny burping sound three times.

Tiger Rock laughed. "Right back at you."

"You understood that, uh, him?" Kai asked

Tiger Rock nodded. "Sure. I know all kinds of languages. If it exists, I can learn it."

Kai walked down the hall, looking left and right, his mouth open in wonder. Tiger Rock strode along next to him. At a bend in the hall, Tiger Rock once again gripped Kai's arm, harder than before. Kai winced a little but didn't squirm.

"It's really cool back here," Kai said. "I never thought I'd get to see what went on behind the scenes. Thanks for showing me."

"Sure," Tiger Rock said. "I like to go all over the place. I can be everywhere."

"That's pretty neat," Kai said.

"Check this out," Tiger Rock said. With his free paw, he pointed at a gleaming silver, circular slide that wound around a metal platform lift, which looked like a moving staircase, sort of like an escalator except none of the steps were attached to one another, or to anything else. They seemed to hover in the air. Each step ascended diagonally to an upper floor Kai couldn't see.

The slide, at first, was empty. Then an animatronic rabbit that looked like a futuristic relative of the Fazbear character Bonnie came skimming down the slide.

Tiger Rock laughed his bass, vibrating laugh. "This is how the performers, like me, and the worker bots get around behind the scenes. It's as good as any of the rides, don't you think?"

Kai grinned and nodded. "The slide looks fun."

"It is. But so is the super slide for Pizzaplex visitors. It's not solid. You ride a slipstream. Wanna try it?"

"Sure!" Kai said.

"All righty, then," Tiger Rock said.

Tiger Rock turned to lead them back to the Pizzaplex's main walkway, and when he did, Kai pulled his arm from Tiger Rock's grasp. It wasn't the robotic tiger's fault—he probably didn't know his own strength—but Tiger Rock's clamp-like grip hurt.

Tiger Rock glanced at Kai several times as they walked back down the hallway. The tiger seemed to be obsessed with Kai's arms, as if he was trying to figure out how they worked or something. Kai considered asking about it, but he felt like the question would be strange. He decided to pretend that Tiger Rock's scrutiny wasn't unsettling, and he didn't ask about it.

Tiger Rock kept his long metal arms at his sides until they reached the main part of the Pizzaplex again. As they stepped into the crowd, though, Tiger Rock once again took Kai's arm. And *ow*, it felt like Kai's arm was caught in a vise. The pressure of Tiger Rock's thick metal fingers was even stronger than it was before.

Tiger Rock was now yanking, just a little, on Kai's arm. Kai wasn't sure why Tiger Rock felt he needed to do that. Kai was keeping up with the tiger; he didn't have to be dragged along like an uncooperative little kid.

Kai's arm was really starting to hurt. But he still didn't say anything. *Go with the flow*, he told himself.

Overall, Kai was having a great time. He was loving all the glitz in this Pizzaplex of the future. It was like being in the middle of a dazzling light show.

Whereas the Pizzaplex of the present was filled with neon and LED lights, the future Pizzaplex's lights were holographic. All the colorful accent lights and lit-up signs weren't attached to anything. Like the steps and the trampoline, they seemed to be suspended by nothing, wafting in the open space like glittering specters. It was beyond cool.

Tiger Rock squeezed Kai's arm harder. Kai gasped and tried to pull away. Tiger Rock hung on, even tighter.

This is getting a little annoying, Kai thought. *Not to mention weird*. Kai wondered why the VR program would include an animatronic that would hurt the user's arm. It didn't seem right.

"We're almost to the slide," Tiger Rock said. "I'll get you to the front of the line."

Tiger Rock wrenched on Kai's arm. Tears springing to his eyes, Kai had no choice but to go along. If he'd tried to resist Tiger Rock's forward motion, Kai was afraid his arm would have been pulled from his shoulder socket. As it was, he was going to have a huge bruise on his bicep.

"Here we go," Tiger Rock said. He manhandled Kai toward more air-stairs, which led to the top of a prism-shaped structure. The prism shot a rainbowlike refraction similar to a stream of water from its uppermost point, and that stream carried the slide's riders, as if on invisible, levitating carpets, down the side of the prism to land at its base.

Tiger Rock compressed his paw around Kai's arm, and Kai felt something pop in his bicep. Okay, that was it.

"Let go of me!" Kai yelled.

The other kids standing in line to ride the slide whirled around to stare at Kai, and Tiger Rock was distracted. Kai took advantage of the moment and wriggled his way free.

Before Tiger Rock could reach for Kai again, Kai dove for the top of the slide. He had a sudden, compelling need to get away from the tiger. He wanted to be done with Tiger Rock.

A kid wearing a T-shirt that featured a too-realistic, in-motion charging bull was about to start his slide, but Kai, tossing aside all his manners, shoved the kid out of the way. "Hey!" the kid protested. Ignoring the kid, Kai threw himself onto the slide.

"That-a-boy, Kai!" Tiger Rock called out.

Kai looked back over his shoulder. His heart sunk.

Tiger Rock was zipping down the slide after Kai. He was only a few feet away.

A few feet, though, was a few feet. Kai figured he'd have enough of a head start to get away from the grabby tiger.

As he slid, Kai felt a little bad that he was trying to ditch Tiger Rock. He didn't get the feeling that Tiger Rock was mean or anything. The robotic tiger probably didn't even know he was hurting Kai. But he *was* hurting Kai, and Kai didn't want that strong metal paw on his arm again. He didn't think he could take it.

Almost to the bottom of the slide, Kai scanned the crowd at the base. He spotted an opening, and he figured he could shoot through it. The entrance to Gator Golf was just beyond the crowd. If this version of Gator Golf was similar to the present-day one, he figured he could hide somewhere among the mini golf course's jungle-themed obstacles. Some of them, he remembered, were pretty substantial. The course also had a back entrance that led to a hallway with restrooms and a shortcut to the main dining room. Once there, Kai could get lost in the bigger crowds.

Kai hit the bottom of the slide, staggered for a second, then caught his balance and darted through the cluster of kids near the slide's base. As planned, he scooted into Gator Golf and shot toward the course.

Although this future Pizzaplex's Gator Golf was similar to the one in the present, its jungle theme included moving animals and reptiles. Obviously animatronic (because who would put real anacondas and jaguars in with little kids?), the creatures in Gator Golf were the course's obstacles. They were, as Kai had hoped, large.

But they were moving. That meant that to hide himself, Kai had to keep up with the predators' motions.

Kai jumped from predator to predator until he spotted a Pizzaplex employee, a young brunette with a ponytail. The woman was cleaning up a stain on one of the greens.

"Can you help me?" Kai asked, panting. "One of the animatronics hurt my arm, and—"

The ponytailed employee flashed Kai a smile, stood, and hurried away. "Have a great time today," she called out as she went past.

Kai frowned but quickly sought out the next obstacle. As he huddled behind a crouched jaguar, he surveyed the golf course. He hunched over when he spotted Tiger Rock scanning the area.

The jaguar shifted its legs, and Kai knew it was going to leap to another spot. Kai readied himself, and when the jaguar moved, Kai did, too. He ran as fast as he could to duck behind a coiled anaconda.

Near the giant snake, a young couple was setting up to play the hole. Kai raised his head just a little.

"Excuse me?" he whispered. "But could you help me? Maybe call someone? One of the animatronics—"

The young couple, their yellow swirling outfits as bright as the sun, hit their balls with lit-up oddly curved clubs. Then they walked away from Kai.

The program wasn't allowing Kai to get help. *No wonder*, Kai thought. The VR program was an illusion in his own mind. It wasn't going to be reactive to his needs.

For the next couple minutes, Kai felt like he was in a fever dream. He was light-headed, and sweat was beading on his forehead. Although everything around him felt solid enough, it seemed to waver in his vision, blurring and deconstructing and then coming back together again.

My time has to be up soon, Kai thought, as he caught yet another glimpse of Tiger Rock's intense gaze scouring the golf course. *Please let the timer go off soon.*

Moving as if in a dizzying hallucination, Kai began to flit this way and that, ducking one second and crawling the next. His movement felt disjointed, almost like he wasn't the one controlling what he was doing. He felt like a puppet on a string, being led from one position to the next. But he *was* the one in charge. It was his will to keep away from Tiger Rock. Kai was calling the shots, even if it felt like he wasn't.

Ignoring the odd way his body felt, Kai kept sprinting around. As he did, he kept an eye on Tiger Rock, who was shadowing Kai all too closely.

Kai's bicep was throbbing. He was pretty sure Tiger Rock had torn a muscle in his arm. How much worse would Kai be hurt if Tiger Rock got his paw on Kai again?

Kai dove behind a black crocodile that was trundling across the green on the ninth hole. *Did Tiger Rock see me?* Kai wondered as he tried to flatten himself to stay hidden by the creeping metal reptile.

Kai risked raising his head just a little. He gasped.

He was looking right into Tiger Rock's mismatched eyes. He was just a couple feet away.

"Are we playing hide-and-seek?" Tiger Rock asked. "I know how to play. I learned a long time ago."

Kai yelped, stood, and ran. He galloped toward Gator Golf's back entrance and shot into the back hall.

Checking over his shoulder, Kai didn't see Tiger Rock, so he dashed into the men's restroom. As sci-fi-ish as the rest of this future Pizzeria, the restroom had faucets suspended in midair, which flowed into a glass trough. Beyond the trough, the restroom contained silver pods instead of stalls. The open pods had no doors that Kai could see, but given that a couple of the pods were solid, he figured the doors were designed to appear when you entered the pod.

Kai rushed past the glass trough and flung himself into one of the silver pods. As he'd hoped, the pod's opening closed, and a shiny silver surrounded him. He ended up in a small enclosure that could have doubled as a small spaceship—minus the polished silver toilet.

Kai looked down at the black-and-white tiled floor (a floor that looked comfortingly similar to the one in the present-day Pizzaplex) and noted with relief that the pod's walls reached all the way to the tile. Good. Tiger Rock wouldn't be able to see Kai's feet.

Kai looked up. His chest tightened. The walls didn't go to the ceiling. They curved inward to create a lip about a foot from the satin-like, white interlocking beams that crisscrossed overhead. Kai stared up at the gap. Could he climb up there and get away if he had to?

Kai pressed himself back against the wall behind the toilet. He tried to catch his breath as quietly as possible.

Come on, ding! he begged. The VR booth's timer had to go off soon. It felt like he'd been in the future Pizzaplex for ten hours instead of ten minutes.

Kai closed his eyes and imagined being out in the familiar, present-day Pizzaplex. He thought about his friends. He'd see them again in no time. This would be over soon. It had to be.

A thud vibrated the pod wall. Something scraped in the pod next to Kai's.

Tiger Rock!

Kai looked up. What if Tiger Rock came down through that opening? If Kai stayed where he was, he'd be trapped.

Kai looked at the pod wall in front of him. How did it open?

He stepped forward, and nothing happened. He put his hand against the pod's wall. And the pod opened. He exhaled in relief.

Kai scurried through the opening on his tiptoes. Thankful he was wearing cork-soled shoes that didn't squeak, he ran toward the restroom's exit.

Glancing over his shoulder, Kai saw that the pod next to him was closed in. Hopefully, Tiger Rock was still in there, trying to sneak up on Kai.

Kai reached the restroom door and pushed it open. Stepping into the hall, he trotted toward the main dining room. It was just around the corner.

Kai picked up his pace. Checking over his shoulder, he was relieved to see Tiger Rock wasn't behind him.

Kai rounded the corner.

"There you are!" Tiger Rock said as he reached for Kai's arms.

Kai shrieked just as Tiger Rock's paws clamped over his biceps. Red-hot pain shot up into his shoulders.

Ding!

Kai blinked and looked around.

He was in the VR booth sitting in the golden chair.

Kai reached up and felt the mesh headband. He ripped it off his head. His arm hurt when he moved it. Kai pushed up his sleeve and studied his bicep. It was bruised.

Shivering, Kai rubbed his arm. He stood and hurried out of the booth.

Kai looked around and spotted Asher and Todd, who were sitting cross-legged near the booth, talking about whether bologna went better with mayonnaise or mustard. Beyond his friends, the VR attendant was chewing on a cuticle and watching a cute blonde walk past the booth.

Kai hurried over to the attendant. "Excuse me, sir?"

"Hey, there you are," Todd called out. "We decided to skip the booth. We're hungry."

Kai ignored Todd and tapped the long-haired guy on the arm. The attendant looked down at Kai and frowned.

"What?" the guy asked.

"Um, I think there's something wrong with the VR booth," Kai said. "One of the animatronics hurt my arm. See?" He held out his arm.

The attendant raised a scraggly black eyebrow and curled his thin lip. He clearly didn't believe Kai.

Kai opened his mouth to say more, but then he shrugged. "Never mind," Kai said.

What was the point in trying to convince an employee who clearly wasn't going to believe anything Kai said? Kai was just glad to be out of the booth.

He turned away from the attendant and went over to his friends. "I want to go home," Kai said.

"Huh? We just got here," Todd protested.

"Sorry. But I don't feel good." Kai massaged his arm again, but he didn't say anything about it to his friends.

"I'm cool with leaving," Asher said. "We could rent a movie or something."

"Yeah, let's do that," Kai said.

"Should we do sci-fi or action?" Asher asked.

"A spy movie," Todd said, giving in to his friends. "I just read a book about spycraft."

"Action movies are more interesting than spy movies," Asher said.

"In what universe?" Todd asked.

And they were off and running. Kai tuned out their argument. Any movie would be fine with him. As long as it didn't have any tigers in it.

On Saturday evenings when the weather was clear (all year, winter included), Kai's family hung out by the firepit in their backyard. Their house was surrounded by tall elms and maple trees, and it backed up to a river. In the backyard, they were sheltered from the rest of the neighborhood, and they were insulated from traffic sounds on the street. Whenever they were tucked in the back, it felt like they were camping.

Kai and his family would sit by the crackling fire, inhaling its sweet smoke, listening to the burbling river and the rustling tree branches. They would talk about the happenings of the previous week, and they'd also tell stories. They'd watch the sunset or they'd stargaze, depending on the time of year.

Kai usually loved the Saturday night tradition. But not tonight. He was too jumpy to enjoy it. He was so on edge, in fact, that tonight he nearly threw his sister into the firepit when she jumped on him. He didn't see her coming, and he felt like he was back in the VR booth when the weight of her little legs landed on his arm.

"Story!" Malia squealed in his ear as she cuddled up against him.

Kai and his dad had been sitting by the fire, silently watching the sun start to sink toward the distant rolling hills. His mom and Malia had been inside fixing Elliot, Malia's favorite stuffed animal, a bedraggled plush elephant (at least it wasn't a tiger). Elliot had "an owie"—a hole in one of his seams.

"Elliot is good as new," Kai's mom announced as she settled into the green Adirondack chair next to Kai's dad.

"Momma did stitches," Malia said in Kai's ear. Her breath was hot and moist, and it tickled the hairs at the back of his neck.

Malia squirmed, settling in. Her wild blonde curls, which always flew in multiple directions around her face if not contained in ponytails or a braid, engulfed Kai's face. Some of the strands got in his mouth. Kai spit them out and pulled his head back to avoid being consumed by her mango-scented hair.

Kai tried to calm his jittery nerves. He wrapped his arms around his little sister and hugged her close.

Unlike other kids Kai knew, who talked about how annoying their siblings were, Kai loved his baby sister. Five years old, Malia was sweet and funny and loving. She was also demanding.

"Story!" she shouted in Kai's ear again.

Every week, Kai and his parents took turns telling Malia long complicated stories about the adventures of Elliot the elephant. This week, it was Kai's turn. He'd been pondering the story he was going to tell all week, but after his experience in the AR booth, he wasn't in the mood to tell it. His story had been about a lion who was stalking Elliot. That was too close to Kai's own experience.

Kai hugged Malia. "I'm sorry, Mally, but I think I'm going to bed." He looked over Malia's flyaway curls. "Mom, could you take it this week? I'll make it up next week."

Kai's mom frowned for an instant. Then her round face returned to its usual relaxed expression. "Of course, Keiki. Are you coming down with something?"

Kai's mom wasn't the kind of mom who hovered or worried. But when she used the Hawaiian word for *child*, Kai knew she was concerned.

He shook his head. "I just feel off today." He shrugged.

Just as Kai hadn't told Todd and Asher what had happened in the VR booth, he hadn't mentioned it to his parents, either. It was just too bizarre to talk about. And it was over.

As one of the Timeless Trio, Kai didn't dwell on the past. What was done was done. He was moving on.

So why am I so uptight? he thought.

Kai ignored his own question as he passed Malia to his dad. Malia, content to wrap her long, skinny arms around her dad's lean shoulders, held up Elliot. She put on a stern face and said in as deep a voice as she could manage, as if she was the elephant, "I want my story next time."

Kai patted Elliot on the head. "I promise you'll have it," he said.

Kai stood. He bent over to kiss his mom, and he accepted his dad's fist bump.

"Are you sure you're okay, son?" his dad asked. The already deep lines between his brows were bunched. Like Kai's mom, Kai's dad wasn't a worrier, but he had a sixth sense when it came to an actual problem. When there was one, he liked being proactive about it, solving the issue instead of fretting over it.

Kai knew his dad's job was stressful, and Kai tried not to add to his dad's load. "I'm fine, dad," he said. "Just tired."

Kai's dad rubbed his wide jaw. "Okay. You'd tell us if something was wrong, right?"

"Sure, dad," Kai said. He hoped that his laid-back parents weren't worried enough to notice he was lying.

As Kai returned to the house, he heard his mom begin a story about Elliot and the hippopotamus he met by the river.

Kai closed the sliding glass door behind him and shuffled down the hallway to his room. As he went, he scanned the family photos that lined the hall. His pace slowed as he gazed at the photos. Seeing all the images of him and his parents and Malia laughing and having a great time helped to erase what he'd experienced in the VR booth.

This is reality, he reminded himself. *Tiger Rock isn't real.*

Kai reached his room. He entered it and closed the door behind him. He leaned against the door and took a deep breath.

It was only nine p.m. Too early to go to bed. But he didn't feel like doing anything.

Kai crossed his tidy room and flopped on the soft gray bamboo comforter spread neatly on his mattress. He looked up at the ceiling and watched the curved blades of his distressed koa fan lazily swirl overhead. The fan made a soft swishing sound that blended with the sound of the breeze in the trees outside his window.

Kai's room was a big square space that had a sisal rug over cork flooring (the same flooring was in the entire house). All his simple furniture was made of reclaimed wood, mostly scavenged from old barns being torn down to build new ones. He liked his rustic platform bed, his large desk and shelves, and the tall dresser that sat between his closet and the picture window that looked out onto the home's side yard. He'd hung a humming-bird feeder in the white pine outside his window, and he spent lots of time watching the colorful little birds whiz-zing in to get some sugar water and streaking away again to disappear into the azalea bushes at the base of the trees.

To Asher and Todd, whose rooms looked like those of normal eleven-year-old boys (overstuffed and messy), Kai was a little strange for caring how his room looked. *Dude, your room is like something in a magazine,* Todd often commented. Todd was fascinated by the mostly bare walls (the only thing Kai had on the walls was a framed photo of his family, a painting of Waianae, one of the inactive volcanos on Oahu, and one of Malia's drawings, which depicted Elliot the elephant giving Kai a ride). Kai's shelves held orderly rows of books, his rock col-lection, and a couple wood carvings—one of an eagle and one of a dolphin. Kai had done the carvings himself. They were a little wonky, but he was happy with them because he was still learning.

Todd was also obsessed with the way Kai's room smelled. Whenever he visited, he sniffed the air like a hound following a scent. The aromas were coconut and lime. Kai's mom made her own cleaning products and chose a scent that reminded her of home.

After watching the fan go around a few dozen times and enjoying the familiar coconut scent of his room, Kai sighed and stood. He crossed to the double-hung window and looked at the hummingbird feeder. Sometimes, his favorite hummingbird, Berry (so named because of his raspberry-red tail feathers), came around in the twilight. But not tonight. The feeder was empty.

Kai's window was partly opened. He pushed it up all the way and leaned out to see if he could spot Berry in the azaleas.

The sun had disappeared behind the hills now, but its glow still remained. There was enough light for Kai to see, although the bushes were already hiding in the coming night's shadows.

No Berry.

But wait. What was that moving just beyond the azaleas?

Something light colored was fluttering. Kai could see the movement through the bushes' tiny leaves.

He squinted and leaned even farther out the window. For reasons he didn't understand, he felt prickles at the base of his neck, and his heart rate sped up.

It's probably just a cat or something, he thought.

The thing, whatever it was, moved again. Kai sucked in his breath.

It wasn't a cat.

It was an owl. A large white owl. The owl was sitting on the ground, angled just a bit away from the side of Kai's house. Its eyes were closed.

The tingles on Kai's neck crept up into his hair. It felt like ants were crawling on his scalp.

A streak of the sun's remaining light stretched through the bushes and landed on the owl, and Kai could see, clearly, that the owl was no normal owl. The light reflected off the owl's feathers.

Owl feathers didn't react to light that way. Metal did.

Kai was looking at a metallic owl, one sculpted like the animatronics in the future Pizzaplex. Kai swallowed hard and watched the owl. It wasn't moving. Was it just some kind of toy or something, or maybe a new garden sculpture his mom had gotten?

Even as Kai dismissed the thought, the owl's head turned, ever so slightly. The head rotated the owl's face so it was directed full-on toward Kai now.

The owl's eyes opened.

Kai cried out and whipped his upper body back into his room. As he did, he bumped his head on the window frame. The impact jarred the window, and it dropped quickly. The window slid completely down, catching Kai's arm between the bottom of the window and the sill.

Because Kai had lunged back through the window so fast, his momentum kept him going, even after his arm got caught. His arm, stationary at the window, didn't come with the rest of his body, which was trying to tumble into his room.

Pain flashed in Kai's shoulder; it felt like his arm was being pried from its socket. Tears sprang to his eyes as he shuffled his feet to get his balance. He grabbed for his dresser, catching himself so he didn't continue to fall away from where his arm was caught in the window.

Gritting his teeth, Kai managed to right himself, and he used his free hand to lift the window off his trapped arm. As soon as the window was up, he retracted his arm and rubbed the spot on his forearm that had taken the brunt of the heavy window's frame. Then he rotated his arm to make sure he hadn't done any major damage to his shoulder. He hadn't. His shoulder was sore, but his arm was moving okay.

For several seconds, Kai clutched his dresser and tried to steady his breathing. His heart was thrumming so loudly that its beat was all he could hear.

When Kai's heart started to settle down, he inhaled and took a step back toward the window. Leaving the window closed, he pressed his cheek to its cool glass and looked down.

The owl was gone.

But Kai didn't feel relief. The unease that had been with him all day had now ratcheted up a notch. No, make that several notches.

Because the owl that had crouched in the bushes below Kai's room was definitely not some toy or yard sculpture. When it had opened its eyes, Kai had clearly seen that the owl had one emerald green eye and one bright blue one.

On Sunday afternoons, Kai and his friends usually went on "quests" when the weather was good. The quests were something Kai's dad had come up with.

How about I hide something somewhere in town, Kai's dad had suggested one afternoon when Kai and Asher and Todd were hanging around, bored, complaining that they had nothing to do. "I'll give you a clue that will lead you to another couple clues," Kai's dad continued, "and you can follow the clues to find the treasure."

Todd, whose own parents were total workaholics who tended to ignore their only child most of the time, had thought this was rad, and Asher had gotten into it, too. That day had started the regular routine they followed now.

Kai's dad was a genius with clues. They had to ride their bikes all over town to find the next clue and the next until they found "the treasure," which would be anything from cookies to concert tickets to a CD. Once, when the clues were really hard, they'd found three fifty dollar bills in a little wooden chest hidden in a nook at the base of the clock tower in the town square.

Kai was still jittery the day after he'd seen the owl. He had gone straight to bed, but he'd lain awake for a long time before finally drifting into a restless sleep. All night long, the owl had haunted his dreams, so much so that Kai had used his "Wake myself!" trick three times. His eyes were scratchy from lack of sleep when he met Asher and Todd on his front porch to study the first clue of the day's quest.

It was a nice day. Spring had finally settled in for good, and the days were getting warmer. The soft blue sky overhead held wispy white clouds. Normally, Kai would have been happy to be outside on a day like today. But right now, the open sky somehow felt threatening. He felt exposed. He kept rotating his head, searching the neighborhood for anything that seemed out of place.

Kai didn't see anything that shouldn't have been there. The mostly one-story houses that lined his narrow street looked as they always did on a day like today, their windows sparkling and their dark roofs shimmering in the sun. The bushes were thick and healthy. The driveways held the usual array of sedans and SUVs. As was common on weekends, several people were mowing their lawns. A few children played in their yards or ran up and down the sidewalks. The air smelled like fresh grass clippings, and the screams of little kids pierced through the roar of lawn mower engines.

Kai forced himself to pay attention to his friends. He needed to forget about the stupid owl and stop looking for things that weren't there.

Todd, who clutched the tiny scrap of white paper that held their first clue, frowned at it. "What does, 'Hey, you don't want to bail on this one!' mean?" he asked.

Kai had no idea, and his mind was too fuzzy to try to figure it out. He shook his head and waited for Asher to come up with something.

Asher chewed his full lower lip for several seconds. He muttered to himself under his breath. Then he snapped his fingers.

"It's Old Man Gruber's place," he said.

"Huh?" Todd said. He unwrapped one of the caramel candies he often had stuffed in his pockets. He popped it in his mouth and held out another couple wrapped ones. "Want some?" he said around the candy in his mouth.

Asher and Kai shook their heads.

"Old Man Gruber doesn't bale his hay," Asher explained. "You know how he just puts it in mounds in his fields?"

Todd nodded. Then he shook his head. "How do you know the clue's supposed to take us to Old Man Gruber's place. This time of year, a lot of hay isn't baled yet. The clue could mean any one of a dozen farms."

"Too random," Asher said. "Kai's dad wouldn't send us to every farm with unbaled hay. Old Man Gruber is known for his unbaled hay."

"I think you're assuming too much," Todd said. "And you know what they say about assuming."

"You're assuming I care what you think," Asher said.

"Hey," Todd said.

"Exactly," Asher said.

Kai wasn't in the mood for Todd's and Asher's bickering. "Come on," he said. "Let's go see what we find at Old Man Gruber's. He has that little stand next to the road, where his daughter used to sell flowers. That would be a good place to hide another clue."

Todd chewed his caramel with his mouth open and thought about it. He shrugged and nodded. "Why not?"

Asher rolled his eyes. All three boys went for their bikes, which leaned against the slender porch railing that ran along the front of Kai's family's house. They all put their feet on their pedals and coasted down the driveway to the street.

Old Man Gruber's farm was only a couple miles from Kai's house. It was a straight shot down the street and then onto one of the back roads that crisscrossed the farms that surrounded the town. As they rode their bikes over, Kai lagged even farther behind than usual.

His mind was not even remotely on the quest. His focus wasn't on pedaling his bike, and he wasn't noticing much about the houses and yards they were passing. He was back to thinking about Tiger Rock. And the owl.

Kai remained lost in his thoughts until they started to pass the last house at the end of the street before turning onto the road leading to Old Man Gruber's place. This house belonged to Mrs. Nelson, a widow who liked to be sure everyone knew she was proud of her thick green lawn, her "prize-winning" flower beds, and her perfect white picket fence.

Kai was pedaling past that fence when he spotted something crouched near one of the posts. He slowed his bike, afraid he was seeing the metal owl again.

When Kai dropped his speed, though, he realized that the lump at the base of the fence board wasn't an owl. It was a cat.

But it wasn't a real cat.

Kai's feet came off the pedals, which whipped around and smacked his calves. He jerked the handlebars as he stared at the cat, and his bike careened off the road.

Only just aware that he was losing control of the bike, Kai kept his gaze on the cat. He could tell it was made of the same detailed metal he'd seen on the future Pizzaplex's animatronics and on the owl in his backyard.

As Kai gaped at the cat, it turned its head. Like the owl—and like Tiger Rock—the cat had one green eye and one blue eye.

Kai's breath caught in his throat, and his left hand lost its grip on the handlebar, so only Kai's right hand squeezed the brake handle when he involuntarily clutched at it. Kai's front wheel locked up, and the bike flipped, sending Kai head over heels into the picket fence.

Kai's left arm shot between two of the fence boards, and his bike came down on top of him. Kai's head grazed the fence boards, and his knees skinned the concrete in front of the fence. Kai got a nose-full of the strong fertilizer Mrs. Nelson used.

Stunned, Kai lay still for several seconds.

"Whoa!" Todd's voice rang out. "Are you okay?"

Kai closed his eyes. He did this partly because of the pain in his head, his arm, and his knees, but mostly he was closing his eyes because he knew he'd landed near the cat, and he didn't want to see it.

Kai heard the sound of bike wheels speeding over concrete. Then he heard the squeak of Todd's brake. After that came the clatter of bikes hitting the ground.

Kai opened his eyes as his friends reached him. Todd leaned over and grabbed Kai's right hand. He tried to hoist Kai up from the ground.

A sharp pain shot through Kai's arm, and he cried out. The pain worsened as Todd tried even harder to lever Kai up from the ground.

"Ow!" Kai screeched.

Todd kept pulling.

"Stop!" Kai yelled. "Stop it! That hurts!"

"Sorry," Todd said, panting. He dropped Kai's right hand.

"His arm's stuck between the fence boards," Asher told Todd as he shifted Kai's bike away from him. "You need to work his arm free *carefully*."

Todd dropped to his knees next to Kai's trapped arm. Kai felt the bike's weight come off his body, and before Todd could "help," Kai turned so he could pull his own arm out from between the boards.

Kai's right shoulder was still sore from the wrenching it had gotten the night before. Now Kai's left arm was screaming as loudly as his right arm had when it had gotten caught in the window.

"Ow," Kai said again. He gingerly rotated his arm and rubbed his shoulder.

"What happened?" Todd asked. "We were up ahead. I didn't see."

Kai wasn't about to describe what had really happened. "It was a cat," he said vaguely.

Todd nodded. "Figures. Cats are menaces."

"They are not," Asher said. "Cats are great."

"Whatever," Todd said. "Everyone knows dogs are better than cats."

"Dogs are stupid suck-ups," Asher said. "Cats are independent."

Todd had some comeback for that, but Kai tuned him out as he carefully got to his feet. His friends continued their cat versus dog argument, one that Kai had heard many times before (Todd had a dachshund and Asher's family had two cats). Kai ignored them and bent over to check his bike. It seemed to be okay.

"I'm going to head back home," Kai said, interrupting Todd's rant.

Asher looked at Kai. "Yeah, that's a good idea. You've got a bump on your head there and your knees are bleeding."

Asher started to turn his bike to go with Kai. Kai shook his head.

"You guys don't need to come back with me," Kai said. "Go ahead and finish the quest."

"You sure?" Asher asked.

Kai nodded. He could feel tears welling, and he didn't want his friends to see them. He turned away from them. "I'm sure. Go on and find the prize."

Kai quickly wiped his eyes. He turned back to face his friends.

Asher and Todd exchanged a look, then they shrugged. "If you say so," Asher said.

Asher and Todd got on their bikes and headed down the street. Kai watched them go, then he started walking his bike home. As he went, his arm continued to throb . . . and his mind continued to replay the image of one green eye and one blue one.

On Monday just before noon, Kai and his friends got out of English class and set off to get their lunch. Kai wasn't really hungry, but he was happy to be out of the classroom. The crowded room with its desks crammed too close together had felt like it was pressing in around him during the whole class. He'd tried to ignore that feeling, so instead he'd spent most of English class thinking about Tiger Rock and the metal owl and cat. Now that class was over, he realized he really had no memory of anything his teacher had said. He figured Todd would fill him in later. Todd was used to telling Kai what he'd missed when Kai's mind wandered off.

Now Kai and his friends were being bumped along by a crowd of kids all trying to get to the cafeteria to be first in line. Kai was still lost in his thoughts. He was wondering if there was some ritual that he could find, something that would get the visions he was having—because they *had* to be visions—out of his system.

Although consumed by his mental chatter, Kai could hear Todd and Asher talking as the three boys approached the top of the escalator heading to the main floor of the old brick building. Yet again, his friends were arguing.

"It's not a stupid assignment," Asher said just before they stepped onto the escalator.

"Yes, it is," Todd said. "Write a story about a food that comes to life? What could be stupider than that?"

"I think it's clever," Asher said. "It's like those commercials where they give candy personalities and stuff. I'm going to write about corn. I think corn could have a great adventure."

"That's corny," Todd said. He snorted out a laugh so loud that several kids below them on the escalator turned around and gave him a look. He, as usual, was oblivious.

Kai stepped onto the escalator last, and so he was looking over the top of his friends' heads as they rode downward. Trying to ignore their continued squabble, he gazed out in front of him, expecting to see the huge, paned arched window that dominated the front wall of the school.

When Kai focused on the building's front wall, he did see the big window. But he also saw something else.

Below the window, a new white clock had been installed. Kai frowned and focused on it.

The white clock had a face. Not just a clock face but an actual face. The clock had two eyes, a round black nose, and a wide, toothy smile. It appeared to be made of metal, and the face was outlined in black. The eyes were designed to look like they were closed. There were mechanical dropped lids under feathery black lashes.

When did they put that up? Kai asked himself.

The escalator brought Kai closer and closer to the clock, but because he was going down, he had to tilt his head back to keep his gaze on it. Something about the clock was giving him the heebie-jeebies.

Almost at the bottom of the escalator, Kai craned his

neck to study the clock. Aware that Asher and Todd were stepping off the escalator, Kai prepared to follow them.

And that's when the clock opened its eyes.

By now, Kai shouldn't have been thrown by the sight of one green and one blue eye. But he was, so much so that his legs went out from under him, and he stumbled.

As soon as Kai stumbled, the escalator stair's teeth gripped the hem of his baggy pants. Kai's left pants leg was abruptly snatched up. His leg was jolted backward so violently that he fell forward. Landing on his stomach, flat, Kai hit his chin on the metal grating at the bottom of the escalator.

For three long seconds, the escalator dragged Kai's leg away from him as if the escalator and his leg were a wishbone and someone was trying to snap the V of the wishbone apart. Kai's groin and left hip joint caught fire. It felt like his leg was being torn away from him. He could feel the escalator pulling and pulling and pulling. And then the pulling stopped.

The muscles in Kai's hip and groin were still straining, but at least the strain was now static, not increasing. Kai became aware of shouting, and he felt hands closing over his ankle. "Get me something to cut his pants!" a man's voice called out.

Kai blinked and looked around. He saw his tall, burly history teacher, Mr. Harris, squatting next to him. Mr. Harris was bent over. Kai had a close-up view of Mr. Harris's curly brown hair. Beyond Mr. Harris, several kids were staring down at Kai.

"Way to go, klutz," a boy called out. It was Ron, one of the big kids who liked to make fun of Kai's frizzy hair.

"That's enough," Mr. Harris snapped.

Ron shut up, but Kai could hear the kids' murmured comments. "How do you get yourself stuck on *stairs?*" one girl said.

Kai felt the pressure on his leg let go.

"There," Mr. Harris said.

Wait a second, Kai thought. *Stairs?*

Kai felt Mr. Harris's warm fingers on the skin of his shin, above his sock. Kai pressed his lips together because the skin was tender; it felt burned.

Kai looked past Mr. Harris, expecting to see the escalator's metal stairs. He blinked and rubbed his eyes.

There was no escalator.

Kai had fallen off the last two steps of a *wooden staircase.* The same wooden staircase he'd gone up and down hundreds of times. Kai frowned and looked at the last step of the staircase. It looked like one of the stair tread's boards had come loose. Apparently, Kai's pants leg had gotten caught under it.

Why had he thought he was on an escalator?

"It doesn't look like you're injured too badly," Mr. Harris said. "But let's get you to the nurse's office just to make sure."

Mr. Harris stood and bent over Kai. "Do you think you can stand?"

Kai nodded. His groin and hip were still burning, and his shin was sore, but otherwise, he felt okay. Physically, that is. Mentally, he was on the edge of a total freak-out. He hoped Mr. Harris couldn't tell that Kai was quivering so much that he had to clench his teeth to stop them from chattering.

What was going on? And when would it stop?

★ ★ ★

As soon as Kai got home, he went straight to his room and locked his door.

After Mr. Harris had gotten Kai to the infirmary, Kai's parents had been called. His mom, just coming off her graveyard shift at the ER, had arrived within fifteen minutes and had a brief discussion with the school nurse.

"You probably just have a mild groin pull," Kai's mom had said as she'd driven him home.

Kai spent the entire evening in his room. He'd only unlocked his door three times. He opened the door when Malia got home from kindergarten and marched into his room with an armful of her "friends" (a collection of five plush animals). Malia insisted that Kai line up her toys on top of his dresser.

"They'll help you get all better," Malia said. After she left, Kai locked his door again. An hour later, he unlocked the door so his dad could come in and say hi and check on him.

"I'm okay, Dad," Kai lied to his dad. "I'm just sore."

And terrified, Kai thought. But he wasn't going to say that out loud.

Kai wasn't sure he was hiding his fear all that well, though, given that his dad commented on how pale Kai was and how on edge he appeared to be. "I suppose that's normal after something like this," Dad said, patting Kai's knee. "Just rest up."

The third time Kai opened his door was to let in his mom. She brought him a sandwich before she returned to the ER for another night shift.

After that, when his parents or Malia knocked, Kai

called out that he was resting and wanted to be alone. Thankfully, they let him be.

If only Kai's fears would be that cooperative. He was so scared that he was going to see some metal thing with one green and one blue eye in his room that he was hesitant to keep his eyes open.

After Kai ate, he stretched out on his bed, closed his eyes, and called Todd, who said he and Asher could come over and keep Kai company, but Kai said he was too tired. Not true. He wasn't tired at all. But he was so scared that he knew he couldn't hide it from his friends if they came over to hang out.

"Let's just talk on the phone," Kai said.

"Sure," Todd said. He then proceeded to entertain Kai with all the reading he'd done about stair-related accidents since Kai had gotten his leg caught. "Over a million people a year are treated in ERs for stair-related injuries," Todd told Kai. "So, you're not alone."

"Good to know," Kai said.

After Kai got off the phone with his friends, he lay in bed with his eyes closed. He still wasn't tired, but what if he opened his eyes and something in his room was watching him with one green eye and one blue eye?

Unfortunately, Kai quickly got bored lying in bed with his eyes closed, so finally, he picked one of his handheld video games and kept his gaze squarely on its screen. That kept him safe until bedtime. Then Kai partly closed his eyes while he got ready for bed. He turned out the lights and lay in the dark, stiff and shivering.

The next morning, Kai was startled awake by his dad's knock on the bedroom door. He couldn't believe that he'd managed to fall asleep.

"How are you feeling?" Kai's dad called through the door.

"I'm sore," Kai called back. "Maybe I should stay home from school today."

Kai not only didn't want to face the kids at school, he also didn't want to leave the safety of his room. In his room, he hadn't encountered any of the metal things with Tiger Rock's eyes.

"That's probably a good idea," his dad agreed. "I can rearrange some things and stay home with you. We can play chess or watch a movie."

Kai didn't want to come out of his room, not even to spend time with his dad. "It's okay," Kai said. "I'll be fine on my own."

The previous year, Kai's parents had decreed that Kai was old enough and mature enough to stay home alone during the day. His parents still hired someone to stay with Kai and Malia if they were going to be out late at night, but they let Kai hang out alone after school, and often, they left him in charge of Malia during the day.

"You sure, kiddo?" Kai's dad called out.

"I'm sure," Kai shouted back.

After Kai's dad said good-bye and told Kai to call if Kai needed anything, Malia shouted through the door, "Peter and Marge and Bubby and Frookers and Slowpoke will take care of you. Tell them I said so."

Kai looked over at the plush animals on his dresser. The black penguin (Peter), gray mouse (Marge), white teddy bear (Bubby), red fox (Frookers), and tan sloth (Slowpoke) looked back at him blankly. They didn't look all that concerned about his well-being, but Kai knew Malia meant well.

"Thanks, Mally," Kai called out.

"Luff you!" she sang out.

"Love you, too," Kai answered.

Kai listened to his dad's and sister's footsteps heading down the hall. Malia started singing a song he didn't recognize, and Kai heard his dad laugh. More footsteps. Murmuring. Then the front door thumped. The house was silent. All Kai could hear now was the sound of the occasional passing car, a few crow caws, and the twittering of smaller birds outside his window.

Kai thought about Berry, but he didn't dare glance outside to check the hummingbird feeder. He still didn't think it was safe to look anywhere.

But Kai had to get up. He needed to use the bathroom.

Kai got out of bed and shuffled across his room. As he went, he forced himself to keep his eyelids at half-mast.

Kai made it into the bathroom, did his thing, and returned to his bed. He sat on the edge of his mattress. His shin really smarted where his skin had been rubbed by the escalator.

No. Not an escalator. Kai frowned and replayed the incident at school.

He really had been sure he was going down an escalator. It had seemed perfectly real, even though he knew his school had no escalators.

So, he wasn't just seeing things with Tiger Rock's eyes. He was hallucinating other things, too. But why?

After the owl and the cat, Kai had assumed that what he'd been seeing was brought on by some kind of stress response triggered by the events in the VR booth. But thinking he'd been on an escalator when he'd actually been on stairs was more than that. It was like Kai was confusing physical reality with a virtual one.

Kai inhaled sharply. *What if I'm still in the VR booth?*

Was that possible?

Everything in the future Pizzaplex had seemed so real. There really was no way to tell the difference between the VR experience and everyday life experience. That meant he could still be in the VR booth and not realize it. Until now.

That had to be it! Kai was still in the VR booth. No wonder his arms still hurt where Tiger Rock had pulled him.

So, what now?

Well, if Kai was still in the booth, all he had to do was ride this out. It had to be over soon. Sure, some of his experiences were unpleasant, even painful, but VR tech couldn't hurt him physically.

Out of the corner of his eye, Kai noticed movement on top of his dresser. He turned his head, and his eyes widened. His heart rate doubled in a nanosecond.

Malia's plush toys were moving.

At first, Kai thought some kind of vibration in the house had jostled the toys, but now, he could see that they weren't just shifting slightly. They were moving forward. With purpose.

As Kai looked on in horrified alarm, Malia's plush toys began creeping across the top of his dresser. All five animals had their black eyes riveted on Kai.

Had their eyes been black before? Kai wondered. It didn't matter. The five sets of eyes were glassy black now, and they were all aimed at Kai.

Kai, frozen by fright and disbelief, wanted to run screaming from his room, but he couldn't get his feet to move. And where would he go anyway? If Kai was still in the VR booth, nowhere he went would be safe.

Besides, these were stuffed animals. What could they do to him? He figured he was better off facing them than going out into the house to encounter some new metal, two-color-eyed menace.

Kai remained rooted to his carpet as he watched Malia's furry friends crawl forward. The plush animals had reached the edge of the dresser, and as Kai stared in shock, they each slid down the side of it. When they reached the floor, they continued to advance. Kai's heart battered his rib cage and sweat trickled down between his shoulder blades. He kept telling himself the toys couldn't possibly hurt him.

Bubby, the bear, reached Kai first. He crawled up to Kai, and then, in a flash of movement, he latched on to Kai's foot.

It was too late to run. Bubby had a powerful grip on Kai's foot. The bear was strong. Bubby had the grip of a real bear.

Kai tried to shake off Bubby, but Bubby hung on. Marge, the mouse, reached Kai's other foot. Marge clamped onto Kai's ankle. Slowpoke, the sloth, and Frookers, the fox, started crawling up Kai's legs.

This can't be real, Kai thought. And he remembered his wake-up trick.

"Wake myself! Wake myself!" Kai yelled.

Nothing changed. Kai didn't wake up. Because he wasn't in a dream. He was in a VR booth.

His closet door creaked open. Out of the darkness, Tiger Rock's mismatched eyes emerged, glowing brightly.

"Help me!" Kai screamed.

Tiger Rock didn't move. He remained in the closet, his gaze locked on Kai's arms and legs.

Kai realized pressure was building in his arm and leg joints. He looked down to see that Frookers and Slowpoke were now glommed onto his arms. All five plush animals were working together, intent on ripping Kai apart.

Kai started shaking his arms and legs, trying to dislodge the animals, but they were firmly attached to him. It was like they were glued onto his skin.

Kai screamed as the pain intensified. It felt like Kai's arms and legs were starting to separate from his body.

Tears filled Kai's eyes. He was panting so heavily he was practically hyperventilating. He started to hear a howling sound. It was close. Very, very close. He finally realized the sound was coming from him. He was screaming, keening in high-pitched strident tones that hurt his ears.

This can't be happening, Kai thought.

"No!" he bellowed when a loud crack filled the room. The pain in his hips seared through his entire body.

Kai closed his eyes tight. He shouted, "Wake me!"

When the pain didn't stop, Kai yelled louder. "Wake me! Wake me! Wake me!"

The jagged pangs shooting down his legs eased. The throbbing torment in his shoulders and hips ebbed.

Kai opened his eyes. He looked down.

Although his joints and limbs ached, they no longer screamed. And the attacking plush animals were gone. So was Kai's room.

Anything resembling normal reality was gone, too. Kai found himself in a surreal whirlpool of spinning color and chaotic sound. The color and sound at first appeared random, without structure or meaning. But as Kai concentrated, he began to see filmy images within the churning colors.

There! That was Glamrock Freddy. Kai could see the jagged flash of Freddy's lightning logo. And there. The Pizzaplex spun into view. Its current stained-glass dome rotated like a top and then morphed into the future Pizzaplex's open-to-the-air force field. Suddenly, a nearly transparent Tiger Rock was overlaid on top of all the other colors and shapes. Tiger Rock's sparkling robe wafted around all the sensory input, as if Tiger Rock was embracing everything that was happening. Tiger Rock's green and blue eyes pulsed and glistened. His teeth gleamed.

Kai closed his eyes again. "Wake me!" he screamed as loudly as he could.

He opened his eyes. Instantly, he spotted something clean and clear and curved.

It was the VR booth's glass wall! Or it least it looked like that.

Chanting, "Wake me!" like a mantra, Kai focused on that wall. It was his way out of the topsy-turvy madness he was in.

Kai, ducking his head against the onslaught of sights and sounds, pushed forward. It felt like he was moving through mud. Everything around him clung to him. But Kai ignored the sensations. He put his hands out, feeling for the booth's wall.

It took time to reach and grope and grasp. But finally, he found the wall.

When he did, though, it didn't feel the way he'd expected it to feel. It didn't feel cool and hard, like glass. It felt spongy and malleable, like thick plastic.

Kai grabbed at the squishy material. He locked his fingers around it, and he began pulling at it. Using every ounce of his strength, he started cleaving the booth wall apart, like he was tearing fabric.

Kai wrested the wall apart farther and farther and farther. Finally, with the spiraling mayhem closing in around him, he managed to squeeze himself through the opening he'd made.

A loud sucking sound filled his ears. A gel-like sensation slithered along his arms. As it did, Kai's gaze focused. Instead of seeing distorted shapes, he saw a real person, a little girl with short, wild blonde hair. The girl, holding hands with a bearded old guy—maybe her grandfather— was also holding hands with a strange-looking doll with a bulging eyeball and features that were all wrong. When Kai looked at the freaky doll, his eyes widened.

And then he was free.

He was outside the VR booth.

Kai found himself facing a mass of red-shirted Pizzaplex employees. All of them stared at him like he was an alien. But one of them stepped forward. It was the long-haired attendant Kai had complained to, the one who had acted like he couldn't have cared less. The guy grabbed Kai's arms and pulled him away from the booth.

"Are you okay, kid?" the long-haired guy asked.

"Kai!" Todd called out.

Kai turned and spotted Todd and Asher. They were at the front of a small crowd of people clustered near the booth.

Everyone in the crowd was staring at Kai. And everyone was talking at once.

Kai took a step toward his friends. He was so relieved to see them that he could have hugged them. But he didn't. Todd and Asher weren't huggers. They'd think a hug was weird, and that would let them know how totally and thoroughly traumatized he was.

"What happened in there?" Todd asked when Kai reached him and Asher. "What did you see?"

Kai shook his head. He felt feverish and dizzy.

Asher, slightly more sensitive than Todd, must have noticed Kai's disorientation. He took Kai's arm.

"Come on. Let's get away from this crowd," Asher said.

"Why's everyone here?" Kai asked.

"The booth locked up," Todd said, his voice pitched high. "You were in there for five hours! They couldn't get you out."

Five hours, Kai thought. No wonder the experience went on and on and on. He could see how five hours in a VR booth could feel like three days in what he'd thought was his real life.

Kai looked back at the booth. He blinked and frowned when he saw that the booth's *glass* door was open. Kai hadn't pushed through plastic as he'd thought. He'd simply stepped through the normal VR booth door.

"They couldn't even get into the booth to try to get you out," Asher clarified. "They called in all their best techs, but the booth wouldn't open."

"Why didn't they break it?" Kai asked, thinking about how it had felt like he'd peeled the booth's walls apart.

"It's apparently made of some kind of special glass, like bulletproof or something," Todd said. "They were talking about how to destroy it without hurting you when the door opened and you shot out of there. How'd you do that?"

Kai shook his head and shrugged. The shrug made him groan.

Kai's arms and legs ached something terrible, and his joints were inflamed. But he looked down and saw to his relief that everything seemed to be in one piece.

It was over.

Kai exhaled heavily and turned away from the VR booth. "Let's go home," he said.

"The Pizzaplex people may want to talk to you," Asher said. "They'll probably need to ask you questions about what you experienced so they can troubleshoot what went wrong."

"They can talk to me later," Kai said.

But he hoped they wouldn't. All he wanted to do was go home and pretend that the VR booth didn't exist. He wanted to forget everything about future Pizzaplex and Tiger Rock and the rest of it.

He just wanted to get on with his everyday *real* life.

If Kai had been able to choose, he would have gone straight home from the Pizzaplex and gone to bed. He felt like he'd been up for three days straight. His eyes burned. He was sore all over, and his brain was so foggy that he could barely remember who he was.

But going to bed in the afternoon would have let his parents know that something weird had happened. There'd have been a lot of questions, and he wasn't up to answering them. So, he'd sucked it up. He'd put on a smile and gone about the rest of his day as if it was a normal one. That even included the Saturday storytelling by the firepit.

The storytelling had been the hardest part of the day. He'd told Malia a disjointed, twisty story about how Elliot and a camel had to go into tunnels to rescue a meerkat that had gotten stuck in a cave, but Kai had been barely keeping it together. He knew, as he talked, that nothing he was saying made any sense. His dad's raised-eyebrow expression and his mom's amused grin combined with Malia's crumpled brow let Kai know that his story was a big fat fail.

Somehow, though, Kai got through it. He even managed to hang on long enough to lead Malia inside and help her get ready for bed. Once she was settled, Kai finally went to his room. Five minutes later, he'd brushed his teeth and pulled on the gray T-shirt and sweats that he slept in.

Kai settled in under his cool comforter. Finally, the day was over. He could put the whole experience behind him.

At first, Kai wasn't sure what had awakened him. His eyes popped open of their own accord and he stared into the darkness that shrouded his room.

Kai's room wasn't completely black. A partial moon cast a pale-yellow glow in through the window; he hadn't bothered to pull his shade before he'd gotten into bed.

Kai lay still. He listened. Why was he wide-awake?

An owl hooted outside. Kai stiffened. He could feel his pulse at his temples. His blood was pumping quickly. Kai's stomach clenched.

Kai thought of the metallic owl he'd seen beyond the azalea bushes when he was in the VR experience. At the time, of course, he hadn't known he was still in the VR booth, and the owl had seemed as real as Kai's sister and parents had seemed. As real as *everything* had seemed. But it hadn't been.

And Kai had nothing to be scared of now. He wasn't

in the VR booth anymore. He was in his home, in his *real-life* bedroom.

The owl hooted again, and Kai gasped. His pulse quickened even more. He was suddenly cold and shivering, as if the temperature had dropped thirty degrees.

Kai clutched at his comforter. He was tempted to pull it up over his head, but the idea of not being able to see what was around him was even more terrifying than feeling exposed.

"It's just a normal owl," Kai said. His words sounded unnaturally loud in the night's silence.

The owl hooted a third time. Kai started trembling.

The trembling was the last straw.

"Get a grip!" Kai chastised himself.

This is stupid, Kai thought. *I'm not in the VR booth. I'm at home.*

Kai rolled onto his side and reached up to adjust his pillow. Okay, so he'd heard an owl hoot. That wasn't weird. He didn't hear owls hoot very often, but once in a while he did. A hooting owl wasn't anything to get excited about. And in the VR experience, the owl he'd seen hadn't even hooted.

So there, Kai thought, satisfied that he'd tamped down his fears. He closed his eyes and willed himself to return to sleep.

Sleep, however, wouldn't come back. Kai's pulse rate wouldn't settle either. He lay on his side listening to the *thp, thp, thp* of his pulse *pit-pat*ting at his temple.

After only a minute or so of that, he couldn't take it anymore. It was like listening to a dripping faucet and feeling the drips on his forehead at the same time.

Kai sat up. He exhaled loudly, exasperated.

"You're being silly," Kai told himself.

Kai wasn't about to let one too long VR experience make him mad, not even for one night. So, he threw back his comforter and swung his legs out of bed.

Kai strode over to his uncovered window. He looked out into the night.

The moon's soft radiance pooled in the open space in front of the pines and the azaleas. The muted light revealed just what Kai had told himself he'd find: nothing. The side yard outside his window was as peaceful and empty as it should have been.

No. Wait.

At the edge of the moon's light, something moved in the nearest azalea bush. Kai frowned.

Kai was tempted to go back to bed and pretend he hadn't seen anything. Then he shook his head. Nope. He needed to put this fear in its place right here and right now.

Kai reached out and pushed up his window.

The cool night air rushed into Kai's bedroom. A gentle breeze rippled the sleeve of Kai's T-shirt. Kai inhaled the air's crisp scent.

See, Kai thought. *Normal. Everything was normal.*

Whatever was in the azalea bush moved again. Kai squinted, but he couldn't make out what it was.

He sighed. He wasn't going to get back to sleep if he didn't satisfy himself that whatever was in the bush was something natural, something not the least bit threatening.

Kai braced his palms on the windowsill and leaned forward so he could get a better view of the rustling branch. He spotted a small, white owl, peering through the azalea's shiny leaves. It was an average, unremarkable, *feathered* white owl.

Kai blew out a long breath of relief. His shoulders relaxed. His pulse slowed. He shook his head and grinned at his silliness.

The owl lifted off and flapped its wings. In the middle-of-the-night hush, Kai could hear the whisper of the owl's feathers as they beat the air. The sound was comfortingly ordinary.

Kai started to pull his head back into his bedroom.

And that's when the night stopped being ordinary.

Erupting from beneath the window like a spouting geyser, Tiger Rock shot up into view, his glittery robe spread wide around him like giant owl wings. Kai didn't even have time to react before Tiger Rock reached for him.

Tiger Rock's sharp-clawed paws latched onto Kai's arms, one paw on each forearm. The pressure was harsh and piercing. Kai wanted to scream, but he couldn't. It happened too fast.

In one, supernaturally strong heaving motion, Tiger Rock jerked Kai's arms out and away from his body. Totally and completely *away*. With a squelching wet crack, Kai's arms tore free of their shoulder sockets.

Warm wetness coursed down Kai's sides. He buckled under the intensity of his excruciating pain.

As Kai's legs went out from under him, he stared into Tiger Rock's glowing green and blue eyes. And just before he lost consciousness, Kai watched Tiger Rock— taking Kai's arms with him—vanish into the night.

THE MONTY
WITHIN

THE DRONING BEE LET OUT AN EAR-STABBING SCREECH AND GRABBED KANE BY THE SHOULDERS, HAULING HIM FROM THE SLEEK SAILBOAT THAT WAS CUTTING THROUGH CALM BLUE WATERS UNDER A DAZZLING BLUE SKY. KANE THRASHED, BUT THE BEE HUNG ON, ITS HIGH-PITCHED KEENS DRILLING THROUGH KANE'S EAR RIGHT INTO HIS BRAIN.

Kane kicked at the bee and fell out of bed. The second his shoulder impacted the rough gray Berber rug that did little to soften the hardwood floor under it, Kane realized that the bee wasn't a bee at all. It was his alarm clock.

Kane groaned and scrambled to his feet. Staggering like he had no idea how to use his legs, he stumbled across the room and slammed his palm down on the top of his obnoxious clock radio.

What had he been thinking when he'd put the freaking thing so far away from his bed? Oh yeah, he'd been thinking that if it wasn't all the way over there, he'd hit the snooze button in his sleep and be late for—

Kane blinked and looked at the clock's glowing blue numbers. "Oh crap!"

Totally awake now, Kane whirled and made a beeline for his bathroom. If he didn't get a move on, he'd be late to pick up Sienna. He'd already been late twice this week, which wasn't winning him any happy girlfriend points.

Kane turned the chrome knob on the wall of his white-tiled shower. As the water started to spurt, cold and loud, he remembered that he'd promised Archer he'd look over his school project before Archer caught the bus. The night before, while Kane had been hunched over his black metal computer desk, tapping on his laptop keys as he worked on his senior essay draft, his mother had reminded him about his "big brother responsibility."

"Why can't you look at the project?" Kane had asked, frowning over a sentence that just wouldn't come out the way he wanted.

His mom had sighed so heavily that her spearmint-scented breath had blown Kane's hair down over his fore-head. "What do I know about baseball?" she'd asked. "Or science?" She'd put a hand on one of Kane's hunched-up shoulders. "And besides, it's your opinion that matters most to him."

Still concentrating on his essay, Kane had given in. What other choice did he have?

Archer, a thirteen-year-old nerd who not only was small enough to be a kid half that age but also tended to have the social skills of a much younger boy, too, had enough trouble in the world without being neglected by the brother he worshipped. The whole reason Archer had done his science project on the physics of baseball was because Kane was his high school's star hitter, getting a full ride to the best university in the state because of his .352 batting average and 1.036 OPS. On top of his great hitting, Kane was an outstanding left fielder (he never bragged about it; it was just what it was), his fielding percentage was an impressive .9842. Archer, who couldn't have cared less about sports but who loved science and numbers, thought Kane's stats made him some kind of superhero.

Steam started pouring out of the shower. Kane adjusted the water's temperature and stepped under the pounding spray. He grabbed his shampoo and started lathering up his hair. The shampoo's coconut scent filled the air.

Kane ran through the coming day in his mind. After he looked over Archer's project and raced over to pick up Sienna to get them to school, he needed to talk to Mr. Rivera, his English teacher, about part of his essay. Then he had his morning classes.

At lunch, Kane hoped to grab some time in the school's woodshop. The year before, he'd signed up for shop class so he could learn what he needed to know to help his mom with her DIY projects. He'd been surprised when he'd discovered that he both really liked woodworking and had a talent for it. He was toiling over an extra credit project now that was to double as a surprise for Sienna, and he was grabbing time on it as often as he could.

After lunch, he had afternoon classes. Then he had baseball practice. Following that, he hoped to grab a couple hours to work on his essay. And then he had the date he'd promised Sienna. When Kane got home from his date, Archer, inevitably, would want to hang before bedtime.

Kane rinsed his hair and groaned. "There needs to be two of me," he said aloud.

His words echoed in the big glass-doored shower stall, and he laughed. If his essay thesis was right, there *were* two of him. The problem was that both Kanes shared one body, and that limited what he could get done in one day.

Kane shut off the water and got out of the shower. Drying off as fast as he could, he stepped over to his mirror and wiped away the fog that covered it. Even though he was short on time, he grabbed his hair gel and his dryer. If he had to cram three days' worth of stuff into one day, he wasn't going to do it looking like a slob. Kane—who understood that his dark brown eyes, symmetrical features, wide mouth, and strong jaw added up to what Sienna called "too handsome for your own good"—thought it only made sense to take care of his looks. Just because he was super busy didn't mean he couldn't have swag.

Kane put his elbows on the shiny-red-laminate tabletop of the small corner booth he'd managed to snag even though the Pizzaplex's main dining room was hopping, as usual. LED lights wrapping the booth's purple vinyl seats flickered in constant motion, creating shadows that played over Sienna's freckled face and lit up her intense blue eyes. The table they shared was so tiny that she was only inches away even though she sat across from him.

"So, the way I see it," Kane said, continuing on the subject he'd brought up as soon as they'd slid into the booth, "the second 'person,'" he curled his fingers into air quotes, "that's inside of us is kind of like our very own Alexa or Siri, a non-sentient intelligence that acts like an on-demand computer, sort of a helper or file keeper, basically managing our lives and running the show."

"You're talking about the left brain," Sienna said, her soft, smooth voice barely audible above the rock music blasting from overhead speakers and the rowdy conversation and laughter of nearby diners.

"Right," Kane said.

Sienna raised an already severely arched brow.

Kane laughed. "No. Left. You're right. I mean, correct."

Sienna laughed her deep husky laugh. Kane grinned at her. For a moment, he forgot his train of thought. The only thing he could focus on was how he was head over heels for her.

As usual, Sienna was looking amazing. Sienna's pale skin almost sparkled in the lights. Her dress, the color of the tangerines that grew on the tree in his family's backyard, wasn't fancy, but the way she wore it made Kane feel like he was way underdressed in his jeans and dark green polo shirt. But that was normal. Sienna's idea of casual was several rungs above his.

Although Sienna usually let her shoulder-length strawberry blonde hair hang free, tonight she'd gathered it in a tousled updo that dangled tendrils down over her high cheekbones. Not usually one for much makeup, she'd made an exception to her rule tonight. Her deep-set eyelids were painted with dark blue shadow, and her full lips were slick with pale pink gloss.

"So, you think our left brain is like a computer," Sienna said. "And that means that the right brain is . . ." She raised both of her long-fingered, short-nailed (painted the same color as her dress tonight) hands palms up.

"Our consciousness," Kane supplied. "Basically, it's what makes us human. It's our sentient connection with the world and with each other."

The gangly, curly haired server bopped up to their booth and placed a large pepperoni pizza and a salad on the table. The strong scent of garlic wafted from the glistening red pizza sauce.

"Thanks," Kane said.

Sienna reached out and snagged a large slice of pizza. Folding the slice in half lengthwise, she blew away steam rising from the hot pepperoni slices and gooey cheese. Then she took a huge bite.

Kane grinned. He loved that Sienna ate a lot, and she ate fast. At five feet eleven inches tall, Sienna was on the varsity volleyball team. She was also a long-distance runner and seemed to have a hollow leg as a result.

"Mm, good," Sienna said, after she finished chewing. "Thanks for bringing me here tonight. I know you're super busy."

"Did you think I forgot what today is?" Kane asked.

Sienna, who'd been about to build another big bite, instead smiled at Kane. "Well, you're pretty romantic, but—"

"But nothing," Kane said. "One year ago today, we had our first date."

"At the old Freddy Fazbear's Pizzeria."

Kane nodded and looked around the Pizzaplex's dining room. "This was as close as I could get to re-creating that, since the Pizzeria shut down."

Sienna smiled and reached out to put a cool hand on Kane's forearm. Her fingers were soft and smooth.

Kane reached into his pocket and pulled out a flat rectangular box wrapped in gold paper. "I was going to wait until after dinner," he said as he set it on the table, "but I can't."

"Which part can't wait?" Sienna asked, eyeing the box. "Your computer part or your sentient part?"

Kane laughed. "I'm not really sure. That's the tough part of my thesis. Because our parts usually work together, it's tough to tell which part is running the show."

Sienna snatched up the box. "Well, I don't care. Both of my parts want to open this now."

Pushing aside her unfinished meal, Sienna tore open the gold paper to reveal a red box. She wadded up the paper and threw it at Kane. It bounced off his chest, and he caught it just before it landed on the pizza.

Sienna was equal parts serious and silly. He loved that about her.

She opened the box and let out a squeal that turned the heads of nearby diners. She reached into the box and pulled out a sloth-shaped onyx pendant hanging from a black stainless-steel chain. "This is so cool!" Sienna breathed. "I love it!"

She half rose and leaned across the table to kiss Kane. He did a discreet fist pump under the hem of the checked tablecloth. *Score*, he thought.

In spite of being pretty much as busy as he was, or maybe because of that, Sienna loved sloths. She collected them in all sorts of forms—plush, ceramic, stone, wood, whatever she could find. She claimed that everyone needed a sloth day now and then to stay sane.

Sienna reached behind her to fasten the necklace.

"Well, whichever part of you chose this," she said as she fingered the onyx sloth, "it did good."

Kane finished his senior essay, "The AI Within," just in the nick of time. He turned it in an hour before the deadline. Now all he had to do was rework the essay into the oral report that every senior had to give at the senior thesis assembly the following week.

When Kane and his family had moved to town four years before and he'd enrolled in his high school, he'd been really scared when he'd found out that the school had a tradition of requiring every senior to write a thesis essay and present it in order to graduate. Kane had spent the better part of his high school years worrying about what he'd write when his senior year rolled around and how he'd manage to give a speech about it. Although he had no problem getting up to bat in front of a crowd, he hated having to talk in front of large groups of people.

But earlier this year, Kane had started thinking about the brain, about how the two sides were responsible for different aspects of human functioning, and he'd asked himself how the two sides worked together the way they did. Then he began wondering what would happen if they didn't work together. He got so into the subject that all his worry about the essay disappeared. He became excited about the project, and he found he was even kind of looking forward to giving his oral presentation.

Which was a good thing, because as busy as he was

with baseball and Sienna and Archer and making sure he finished strong in all his classes, the week between handing in his essay and the day of the senior thesis assembly passed in what felt like a nanosecond. Actually, Kane's entire senior year felt like it was racing past. One second, he and Sienna had walked hand in hand down the hall on the first day of the school year, and the next, Kane was standing behind the scarred-wood podium in the school's high-ceilinged, cedar-walled assembly hall.

Kane gripped the podium with both hands and looked out at the rows and rows and rows of burgundy velour-covered seats. Every one of them was occupied by kids and teachers; hundreds of pairs of eyes stared up at him.

Kane cleared his throat and said, "Batter up."

His audience laughed.

Okay, he thought. *That was a good start.* He exhaled and relaxed his fingers so they weren't trying to bore through the podium's sides. He glanced down at his notes, then realized he didn't really need them. He knew this stuff. So, he looked up. His gaze scanned the crowd. He found Sienna, and he spoke directly to her.

"When I," Kane pointed at himself, "am talking to you," he pointed at the audience, "which part of me is talking to which part of you? That question is the focus of my essay."

Sienna smiled at him. She gave him a slight, encouraging nod.

Kane took a deep breath. "Okay," he said, "so I won't throw too many dates at you, because Mr. Freeman and Ms. Boyd do enough of that." Kane pointed at the senior class's two history teachers. They both smiled.

"But I will pitch a couple dates," Kane said. "Don't

worry. There won't be a test on this when I'm done."
Kane enjoyed the chuckle that got him.

"In the late 1700s," Kane said, "a guy named Meinard
Simon du Pui said that humankind was 'Homo Duplex'
because he thought humans had a double brain with a
double mind. Almost a century later, a guy named Arthur
Ladbroke Wigan took that idea further after he watched
the autopsy of a man who was missing one hemisphere
of his brain but could walk and talk and read and write
and do everything he did just like a normal man." Kane
winked at the audience. "He did that before he died,
obviously." Another chuckle.

I'm on a roll, Kane thought.

"If you paid any attention at all in biology," Kane
said, "you know that our brains have two hemispheres,
cleverly named left brain and right brain." More chuckles. "But this guy had been living with just half a brain.
And according to the people who'd known him, he
acted like pretty much any ordinary guy. So, Wigan
concluded that if a guy could function with half a brain,
then half the brain could be one whole mind. This
meant that those of us who have both brain halves have
two minds. He called this the 'Duality of the Mind.'
Kind of mind-blowing, huh?" Kane grinned, and his
audience laughed again.

"Fast-forward to the last century," Kane said. "A Nobel
Prize–winning neuropsychologist and neurobiologist, Roger
Sperry, did a bunch of split-brain studies. Back then, sepa-
rating the two hemispheres of the brain by cutting through
the corpus callosum (the nerve fibers that connect the two
sides) was done for medical reasons, to treat epilepsy, and
Sperry studied how people functioned when their brains

were separated." Kane made a face. "He studied split brains in cats and monkeys, too, but that kind of creeps me out, so I'll stick with what he found in the humans." Another rumble of amusement rippled through the assembly hall.

"The study results are really strange to think about. I'll tell you about just a couple of them. So, Sperry knew that each side of our brains is responsible for the opposite side of our body. This means that your right brain works with the left eye and vice versa. He designed his experiments so he could monitor what each eye saw so he could tell what information was going into the brain." Kane paused. "Are you with me?"

He saw several nods. "Okay," he said, "so one of the things Sperry did was show words to either the split-brain person's right eye or left eye. He found that the only words split-brain people could remember were the ones they saw with their right eye (meaning it was the left brain that was remembering the word; the right brain could not). If Sperry showed two different objects to a split-brain person—one to the left eye only and one to the right eye only—and then asked them to draw what they saw, the participants could only draw what they saw with the left eye (meaning they processed the image with their right brain). What the right eye only saw, the people couldn't draw, but they could describe it with words. Because of this, Sperry realized that the left brain is the part that uses language and speech. The right brain can't, on its own, function in that way. And what's really interesting to me is that whatever word or image was shown to the right eye, if it was then shown to the left eye, the person acted like they'd never seen the word or image before. In other words, each side of the brain was acting as an individual unit, and the other side of the brain wasn't aware of what its opposite was doing. This means that when the two sides of the brain can't communicate with each other, things done by one side of the brain can be done without the other side of the brain even being aware of it. Wild, huh?" Kane saw lots of nods in his audience.

"Sperry did a whole bunch of cool experiments," he continued, "but I won't bore you with them. The important thing about them is that they showed Sperry that people act differently depending on whether their brain halves are connected or not. Basically, when the brain is separated, people have two independent brains with unique personality traits."

Kane looked out at all the faces to see if people were zoning out. Except for a couple of his teammates, who were bent over their phones, probably watching a game, his audience seemed pretty engaged.

"Okay," Kane said, "so I'll tell you about one more person who has written about the left-brain/right-brain stuff, and then I'll tell you what I think and why."

Kane decided the podium made him feel like a stuffy professor, so he stepped out from behind it and just stood at the front of the stage. Seniors were required to dress up for their presentations, so he was wearing a pair of pleat-front navy slacks, a burgundy-and-navy-striped shirt, and a navy tie with tiny white baseballs on it. He'd spent extra time on his hair that morning. He knew he was looking good, but he tried to act like he didn't know it.

"In 1996, a neuroanatomist," Kane said, "Jill Bolte Taylor, who was only thirty-seven at the time, had a stroke, which means that a blood vessel burst in her brain. In Taylor's case, the vessel was in her left brain.

This meant that basically her left brain went offline, and what she experienced made it really clear how the right brain acts without the left brain, which in turn makes it clear how the left brain functions. Taylor, by the way, recovered from her stroke—it took eight years. She wrote a book about what she learned about her brain and how it works. It's called *My Stroke of Insight*, and if you ever want to quit messing with your cell phone or stop playing video games, it's worth reading."

A few kids heckled him from the audience. Kane looked at Sienna. She was smiling.

"What Taylor experienced," Kane went on, "showed Taylor that when the brain is connected and all the neurons are functioning the way they should, it makes us feel like we're having just one cohesive experience of the world. We're not aware that there's a right-brain perception and a left-brain perception. We don't realize that there are basically two parts of us. But there are."

Kane looked out at his audience to see if he still had everyone's attention. Most of the eyes in the auditorium were focused on him. So far, so good.

"When Taylor's left brain wasn't functioning correctly, she was using just her right brain and she not only felt differently, she held herself differently. The way she moved and the expressions on her face were different. For instance, she said that a brow furrow she usually had on her face before the stroke was gone when the left brain was damaged. In other words, when Taylor's left brain was offline, she kind of blissed out. She couldn't do things like talk or function in any sort of get-things-done way, but she didn't care. She said that when she was functioning with primarily her right brain, she was really happy.

What she discovered was that when the left brain was out of the picture, the right brain was super chill."

Another round of chuckles.

"The thing Taylor learned that supports my theory," Kane said in his normal voice again, "is that without her left brain, she had a terrible time trying to communicate with others or trying to get things done. The left brain basically is what allows us to talk and organize and learn and calculate and prioritize. All that stuff that makes us *productive*." Kane put heavy emphasis on the word. "And you know how much our parents and teachers want us to be *productive*." More strong emphasis. Everyone laughed.

"Okay," Kane said. "Enough about Dr. Taylor. Let's get to me and how I think." He straightened his shoulders and pointed at his chest with his thumb as if he was the man. That got him another laugh.

"My theory," Kane said, "is that the left side of our brain is like a non-sentient computer. The right side is our sentience. For those of you who need to expand your vocabulary," Kane winked, "*sentience* means consciousness. And consciousness is basically your awareness of you. It's being clued in to your thoughts and feelings and memories and what's going on around you."

Kane strolled away from the podium and looked out at his audience. "I think of the computer side of our brain as a sort of Alexa or Siri, an artificial intelligence that basically acts as, let's say, the word-processing program and the data-processing program in our minds. It's what keeps us on track so we can get things done. The AI within is what makes us *productive*." Kane drew out the word again. A few people chuckled.

"The thing is," Kane said, "productive is great and all, but Dr. Taylor's experience shows us that the left brain, because basically it is just a biological AI that's running programs instead of being present in the world, can cause all kinds of problems. Back to Taylor for a second. She said she noticed that when her left brain was sidelined, she stopped putting herself down and questioning herself. I'm sure you've all heard the term *negative self-talk*." Several people nodded.

"Well," Kane said, "I think that self-talk comes from the computer part of ourselves. I mean, think about it. Why do we even talk to ourselves at all if there's just one part of us? Who's talking to whom?" Kane paused to give everyone a few seconds to think about that.

"So, imagine if the left brain," he said after his pause, "or what I think of as our inner AI, took over completely. The left brain runs programs based on whatever information it has taken in. What if the information that's gone into your inner computer isn't the best information? What if your storytelling program is running on crap that was put in the system when you were little, by people who didn't know what they were talking about? I mean, our parents and teachers try, but they don't get it right all the time."

Mr. Freeman, the younger of the two senior history teachers—a big dark-skinned ex-football player with massive shoulders—cupped his hands over his fancy-trimmed goatee and shouted out, "Who says we don't?" He gave Kane a smile when everyone in the assembly hall hooted and laughed.

Kane smiled. "Hey, I'm not going to argue with you, Mr. Freeman. I could beat you in a home-run derby, but you'd flatten me in any other contest."

The audience laughed even harder.

Kane waited for quiet, then he went on, "My point is that AI can only use what it's given, and without the balancing force of the right brain, it will contort itself all over the place to fit the data it receives into what it understands, even if what it understands is all wrong. Because of this, I think it's very possible that many of the behavioral problems that people have is a result of the biological AI using bad data. When the AI has bad data, it can turn into something that is harmful to itself and the systems around it."

Kane noticed that a few people in the audience had started frowning at him. He shrugged inwardly. He knew this was where he might go in a direction that not everyone could follow.

"The thing is, though," he went on, "if we could get used to the idea that we have within us these two parts that have totally different agendas and functions, we can be more aware when the computer part starts to lead us off a cliff. I mean, since I started working on this paper, I've noticed that sometimes that computer part of me, the part that runs on what I think I know, really likes to stir up trouble. It can basically be a big drama queen . . . or drama king." He grinned and several people smiled at him.

"Back to Dr. Taylor one last time," Kane said. "When she was recovering from her stroke, basically getting her AI within functioning again, she said she realized that the parts of her that are ones she's not in love with—the stubborn, arrogant, and jealous parts, for instance—are in her left brain. Basically, it's the left brain, that computer part, that can make us act like jerks. There's no question that the AI within does a lot of good. It helps us get dressed in the morning and drive without plowing into people (most of the time)." Another wave of laughter swept through the room.

"But the AI part of our minds," Kane continued, "can also be our worst enemy. My theory is that we all would live better if we had full knowledge of the fact that this non-sentient—and therefore, really, nonhuman—part of us has a lot of control over what we say and do."

Kane returned to the podium and squared himself up behind it. "It all comes down to, 'Thinker beware.' Just sayin'." He stepped back and gave a cocky little bow to make it clear he was done.

And now comes the moment of truth, Kane thought.

As Kane stepped away from the podium, Ms. Stockton trotted up onto the stage. Her back to the audience, she gave Kane a thumbs-up.

He relaxed a little. Even though his talk had gone well—he thought—this was the part of the process that he'd not allowed himself to think too much about.

After every oral presentation, the audience was given the opportunity to offer comments, which didn't necessarily affect the grade you got, but they could be a real ego killer. Kane had seen several of his friends get reamed by their peers.

Ms. Stockton patted her tidy, graying pageboy haircut and straightened the yellow button-down blouse she wore with a navy-blue straight skirt.

The audience had started murmuring while Ms. Stockton took her place on the stage. She rapped on the podium with her large knuckles. The voices quieted.

"Okay," Ms. Stockton said. "Let's have a show of hands. Who buys what Kane was selling? Who believes in the AI within?"

Kane looked out at the audience he'd thought had

been pretty receptive to what he was saying. He expected to see a lot of hands.

But he didn't. Only a couple dozen hands went up, and those were tentative.

Kane forced himself not to slump. But he couldn't contain a sigh of disappointment. His gaze sought Sienna's. Her hand wasn't up. She gave him a "sorry" look and shrugged.

Kane loved that Sienna had her own opinions and didn't just mindlessly go along with him on everything like a lot of his buddies' girlfriends did with their boyfriends. But really? Why hadn't she told him before that she didn't believe his theory?

"I think it's all a bunch of crap," someone called out.

Kane squinted and saw that the speaker was Reg, the football team's starting quarterback. Kane thought of Reg as a pretty good friend.

"Why is that, Reg?" Ms. Stockton asked. "Stand, please."

Reg got to his feet. "Well, it sounds to me like a kind of 'video games cause society's problems' thing."

Kane frowned and made a face. *What?* he thought. He hadn't even mentioned video games.

"Go on," Ms. Stockton said.

"Well," Reg said, running a hand over his dark brown buzz cut, "he seems to be saying that what we're exposed to is what goes into this computer in our brain, and that's what messes us up. It's the same thing that people say about video games."

One of the cheerleaders, Candy, stood. Her blonde ponytail bounced as she nodded. "I agree with Reg," she said. "I mean, Kane was really funny and interesting, and I think he should get a good grade because he obviously did a lot of research and stuff, but it doesn't make sense to me that there's some computer in our head that makes us do bad stuff."

Oh, man, she's oversimplifying, Kane thought. Or had he just not explained himself well enough?

For the next few minutes, while others weighed in with similar comments, Kane told himself that his hurt feelings were just his computer reacting from old programs. He looked out at Sienna and watched her toy with her new sloth pendant. That made him feel good, so he did his best to tune out the rest.

Once the essay assembly was over, there were only six weeks left until graduation. Kane was relieved that the heavy work of his essay was done, but that didn't mean things had lightened up much. He still had baseball practice and games. He still had exams to study for. And he still had Sienna. Kane and Sienna weren't going to be at the same college come fall, and he wanted to spend as much time with her as he could before they separated. They'd decided they were going to try a long-distance relationship, but Kane wasn't sure how that was going to work out.

All of this was why Kane had to work to suppress a groan when Archer started bugging Kane to take him to the Freddy Fazbear Mega Pizzaplex. "But Arch," Kane said when Archer brought it up the evening of the essay assembly, "we've done everything there is to do in that place. Aren't you bored with it by now?"

"Nuh-uh," Archer said as he took a big bite of the tacos Kane had made them for dinner.

Kane and Archer sat outside at the wrought-iron table on the edge of their yard's cedar deck. Kane didn't much like the table because silverware liked to fall through the tabletop's fancy curlicue design, but at least his mom had gotten comfortable cushions for the table's matching chairs. The cushions were bright yellow and red striped, and they reminded Kane a little bit of a circus—and also of the Pizzaplex, actually.

The evening was warm and still. It was so quiet in the backyard that Kane could hear a bee buzzing around his mom's red geraniums.

Archer wiped his wide mouth. "I wanna play air hockey," he said. He took another bite of taco and started talking about air hockey strategies, with his mouth full.

"So can we?" Archer asked, shoving more taco into his mouth. "Play air hockey?"

Kane blinked and realized his inner AI had shanghaied his thoughts. He returned to the present. "Why can't Miles go with you?" Kane asked.

Miles was Archer's one and only friend. It killed Kane that his little brother couldn't seem to make more friends. Archer and Miles got picked on at school all the time.

Kane bit into his own taco. It was a little heavy on the cilantro, but otherwise it wasn't bad.

Kane's dad had left five years before. He was a doctor, and he'd "fallen" for his office nurse. Kane hadn't forgiven his dad yet for leaving Kane's mom. His dad was a jerk.

His mom ran her own interior design company, but now she worked long hours, and Kane and Archer were on their own a lot. So Kane had taught himself to cook. He thought he was getting pretty good at it, too much cilantro aside.

"Miles went camping with his dad and little sister," Archer said, still crunching his taco. He looked up at Kane and grinned, his teeth stained with taco seasoning, salsa smeared over his chin. He wiped at it just before some dripped onto the oversized pale blue T-shirt he wore with baggy jeans. "Please, Kane! We could go after dinner."

Kane took another bite, inhaling the sharp scent of the lime he'd added to the meat. *That was a good touch*, he thought.

"Please," Archer repeated.

Kane sighed. He'd planned on taking Sienna to a movie, but she'd understand if he canceled. She had a little sister. She knew how it went.

"Okay," he said. "Let's do it."

"Yay!" Archer shouted, spewing taco shell bits all over the black wrought-iron curlicues.

There was only so much air hockey a guy could take. After seven games, Kane's wrist was getting tired, and his brain—left or right? He wasn't sure—was tired of listening to the puck clatter into the goal. He was also getting a headache from the blinking lights and the zips and zings and pings and gongs that all the other games emitted in a jumble of sound.

"Let's go get an ice-cream cone," Kane said to Archer.

Archer, who'd been about to start another game, shoved his tokens back in his pocket. "Okay!"

Kane had been pretty sure that would work. Archer loved ice cream.

Kane and his brother wove their way through the other games. They passed the rows of pinball machines, the racing games, the basketball toss, the shoot-'em-up games.

Kane passed a life-size plastic version of Roxanne Wolf as he brushed by one of the racing games. He turned the corner to head toward the arched opening to the arcade, but a flashing orange neon sign brought him to a stop.

The sign read GROUNDBREAKING TECHNOLOGY ALLOWS YOU TO BE YOUR OWN PARTNER! Kane lifted his gaze to the LED lights flashing above the sign. The lights surrounded a flaming orange arcade game front.

Curious, Kane caught Archer's sleeve. Kane pulled Archer toward the machine.

"Where are we going?" Archer asked.

Kane pointed at the new game. It was called Fazcade Tag-Team.

"I want to check this out," Kane said.

Archer squinted at the game's sign. "A new game. Cool. Okay."

They walked over to the entrance of a cavelike enclosure that housed eight easy-chair-like orange vinyl seats, each paired with a fancy bright yellow joystick. The seats sat in a semicircle in front of a massive—maybe eighteen feet by twelve feet—concave screen that made up the cave's far wall. The screen's clarity was so amazing that it could have been a window offering a view of a giant cafeteria, in which a rowdy food fight between Fazbear Entertainment animatronic characters was ongoing. But of course neither the cafeteria nor the food fight was real.

Kane and Archer stepped under the overhang of the cave's entrance and turned to look at the machine's instruction board. Archer read the glowing neon green words out loud. "Are you ready for a food fight? You and your buddies can team up against another group of players on the other side of the Pizzaplex. Pick your favorite animatronic partner and fight side by side with them. How it works: Your favorite Fazbear Animatronic can sync with your mind. Control them with your thoughts and intentions."

Archer looked up at Kane and tugged on Kane's sleeve. "I've never been in a food fight," he said.

Kane hadn't, either. And he didn't think he'd missed anything. But what intrigued him about the game was the idea of working with an AI partner that followed his instructions. It was like a game version of what his essay had been about. He thought it could be a fun way of acting out his theories.

"Okay," Kane said to Archer. "Let's try it out."

Four of the eight seats in the game were occupied. Kane pointed to two empty seats on the far left. Archer grinned and dashed to claim the one on the end.

As Kane settled into the super-comfortable seat, thinking he should get one for his dorm room, Archer fed tokens into the machine. Archer leaned forward and squinted at the small control panel beyond his joystick.

"It looks like we get to choose which animatronic we want to be, and then we're assigned a partner." Archer tapped on the control panel, and a purple-blue animatronic bunny wearing a red bow tie appeared on the big screen. It stood at the edge of the cafeteria, away from the food-fight action.

"I'm Bonnie," Archer said. "Who do you want to be?"

Kane shrugged. He didn't really care. He just wanted to see how the game worked.

"Come on," Archer urged. "Pick one."

"Okay," Kane said. "Orville." Orville Elephant was one of the not-as-well-known Fazbear Entertainment characters; he was in the *Freddy Fazbear's Pizzeria Simulator* game.

Archer giggled as he tapped the keys. "You're big enough to be an elephant," he told Kane.

Kane lifted one arm up in front of his nose and flipped it as if it was a trunk. He made what he thought was a passable elephant trumpeting sound, which earned him a glare from the black-haired girl sitting next to him. He smiled at her, but his charms didn't get past her heavy goth-look makeup and multiple nose and eyebrow rings.

Kane returned his attention to the screen. Now standing next to Archer's Bonnie was an orange animatronic elephant. The elephant wore a purple top hat and had two black buttons and a purple-petaled flower on his chest.

"Looks just like you," Archer said. He snorted and laughed loudly.

Kane grinned and reached for the yellow joystick in front of him. He tested the joystick's maneuverability, and once he had the hang of it, he had Orville pick up a bowl of Jell-O from the array of food on the cafeteria's buffet line. Orville tossed it at Bonnie.

"Hey," Archer said, quickly using his joystick so Bonnie could jump out of the way, "I'm on your team."

"Oops," Kane said. He grinned when Archer elbowed him.

Kane looked at the screen and noticed that Bonnie was now accompanied by the Fazbear character Glamrock Chica, a perky white chick in a pink-and-purple leotard. Orville had been joined by Montgomery Gator, a green alligator with a yellow belly (literally, not figuratively, Kane hoped—he didn't want to go into a food fight with a cowardly gator at his side). Monty had a red mohawk, and he wore a pair of star-shaped sunglasses. Usually suited up in purple-and-green armor, this version of Monty had on a purple chef's apron. Kane was familiar with Monty's character. The gator, in Pizzaplex shows, was the animatronic band's bassist. He was jolly, mischievous, and the most aggressive of the Fazbear Glamrock characters. Monty was often roaring and destroying things. He was also pretty egotistical. When he was defeated in a game, he was known to say, "How can I lose? I'm so handsome!" As a partner in a food fight, Kane figured, Monty would be pretty effective.

"Are you ready?" Archer asked. "I'm going in!"

Kane watched Bonnie and Glamrock Chica charge into the food-fight fray. Kane gripped his joystick, and he and Monty hurtled forward.

The food fight on the screen had obviously been ongoing for some time, and what had originally been a white-walled, black-and-white-tiled-floor cafeteria was now plastered with foods in nearly every color imaginable. A couple dozen animatronic characters were dodging and weaving between overturned tables and scattered chairs, and another dozen were loading up on food ammo from the buffet line.

Kane decided arming Orville was the optimal first move, so doing his best to avoid being pelted by flying spaghetti and sloshed by spurts of thick chocolate milkshake, he had Orville make a beeline for the rows of food. Monty moved in tandem with Orville, as if with one mind.

As they moved on-screen, all the characters shouted good-natured threats and let out exclamations of defeat or triumph, depending on the situation. As Monty and Orville headed toward the food, Monty sang out, "Party time!"

Kane grinned as Orville trumpeted, "Let's do this!" and Monty responded with "Let's have some fun!"

At the buffet table, Monty split off from Orville. "Rock and roll!" Monty thundered as he ran.

Kane manipulated his joystick so that Orville headed for the fruit bowl at the end of the row. Monty went the other way, snatching up a platter of cupcakes and darting into the fray. Other characters scattered as Monty cried, "Run, run, run!" Monty's voice was an amusing mix of mischievous teasing and gravelly bass threat.

Kane left his partner to his cupcake barrage and let himself get totally caught up in the game. And he had a surprisingly great time. Leaping, diving, and rolling the same way he did in the outfield, Kane discovered he was sort of a food-fight phenom. Within minutes of joining in the chaotic mess in the virtual cafeteria, Orville had kicked some serious food-fight butt. Kane watched the other players, and he picked up on their evasive moves. As a result, Orville's orange body got a little stained, but he didn't look as messy as most of the other players' characters did.

Kane was so caught up in what Orville was doing in the game that he didn't pay too much attention to his alligator partner at first, other than trying to protect Monty when the opposing team tried to squirt the gator with ketchup or pummel him with bread rolls. Because the game didn't provide a method of direct communication between team members, Kane figured the best he could do was have Monty's back, and he hoped Monty would have his.

As the game progressed, though, Kane started to notice that Monty, instead of doing his own thing as Orville was doing, was for the most part mimicking Orville's (i.e., Kane's) moves. Once he realized what was going on, Kane started studying Monty. And sure enough, he saw that Monty was not only using moves that were nearly identical to those of other players but he was also using some of Orville's (under Kane's direction) moves, too. Monty began to use both the unique skills that Kane had brought to the game from his baseball experience and also the new skills that Kane had learned as he played.

Interesting, Kane thought. *How did that work?*

Kane moved Orville to a sheltered position behind one of the cafeteria counters. Then Kane took his hand off the joystick and stretched his fingers. He rolled his head on his neck, something he often did on the baseball diamond to make sure he was loose and dialed in to what was going on around him. As his head rotated up, Kane's gaze landed on the game-cave's ceiling, and he noticed a glowing circle, about a foot in diameter, above his head. What was that?

"Get in the game!" Monty's deep voice called out.

Kane refocused on the screen. A Glamrock Freddy was trying to sneak up on Orville with a big bowl of oatmeal.

"Oh, no you don't," Kane said.

On the screen, Orville catapulted from behind the counter and leaped over Freddy. Orville's stumpy elephant legs kicked the oatmeal out of Freddy's grasp, and then the elephant used his more-than-would-have-been-normal-for-an-elephant dexterity to snatch the bowl away from the animatronic bear. He dumped the oatmeal on Freddy's head and then scampered off to rearm himself with more fruit.

As Orville went in the direction of the fruit bowl, Kane noticed that Monty was running alongside Orville. Kane had to send Orville the long way around a tangle of overturned chairs, and as he did, he pondered his next couple of moves. How much fruit should he have Orville try to carry? Should Orville attack or evade next?

Kane was concentrating hard on his strategy, so at first, he didn't notice what Monty was doing. But then he saw that Monty had gone still, as if frozen, on the screen. *That's weird*, Kane thought.

But then a Roxanne Wolf came at him with a sloppy bowl of guacamole. Her partner, the pirate fox, Foxy, flanked her. He was carrying a big basket of tortilla chips.

Kane stopped planning. He moved the joystick and sent Orville into action.

On the screen, Orville dove behind the tangle of chairs and held one up to block the torrent of chips that were directed his way. Next to him, Monty, roaring fiercely, was back in motion again. Monty shouted, "You're in trouble now!" as he snatched up a platter from the floor. Using the platter as a shield, Monty advanced on Foxy and lobbed a bowl of pudding at the fox's head. "Fast and loose!" Monty bayed.

With a rumbling growl, Monty did a little victory dance. "I'm the man!" he crowed.

For the next several minutes, Kane's attention was split. Part of him was playing the game, but part of him was analyzing Monty's behavior. It was really intriguing.

As he played and observed, Kane began to see that whenever he concentrated on Orville's actions, trying to plan out his moves and get all strategic about them, Monty would go still, as if glitching. When Kane took his hand off the joystick and let Orville go idle, Monty would move freely, mimicking Kane's gameplay. It was like Monty was connected to Kane somehow, even when Kane wasn't using the game control.

As he played, Kane frequently glanced up at the glowing golden circle above his head. The light was pulsing a little. Its movement was barely noticeable, but the longer Kane paid attention to it, he realized its fluttering rhythm was irregular. The light's shimmer reminded Kane of the often-sporadic oscillations of brain waves.

Kane frowned. On the screen in front of him, Orville rotated to look at Monty, who, again, turned to stone.

Kane let go of his joystick and craned his neck to look up at the light above his head. *What was that thing?*

Kane felt the muscles in his shoulders tighten as a radical thought popped into his head. He tried to dismiss the thought, but it didn't to go away.

He reviewed what he'd observed in his game. He replayed Monty's moves in his head.

He frowned. What if he was right?

Kane felt a tug on the sleeve of his T-shirt. He blinked and looked to his left.

Archer. He'd forgotten all about Archer.

"Our time's up," Archer said. "I'm ready for ice cream. Okay?"

Distracted by his thoughts, Kane nodded. Archer jumped up.

"That was fun," Archer said.

Kane nodded again as he rose from his seat. He looked up at the circle above his head. Its light was dimmer now, and it was still.

Had it been doing what he thought it had been doing?

Archer,. chattering about throwing french fries and getting hit by hamburger patties, led the way out of the Fazcade Tag-Team cave. Kane followed him, but he couldn't stop thinking about what had just happened.

However strange it might have sounded if he'd said it out loud, Kane was convinced that the Fazcade Tag-Team game somehow took advantage of the very ideas Kane had researched for his essay. He was sure the game had somehow used his biological AI during the game. The way Monty had behaved really seemed like the game had been hijacking part of Kane's mind.

The entire next day, Kane was distracted by the food-fight game. His obsession with it made him miss a good half of what he heard in his classes and caused him to make two stupid errors during baseball practice. At least it was practice and not a game.

When Sienna lit into him for not listening to her when she tried to talk to him about a problem that she was having with one of her volleyball teammates, Kane realized he had to solve the mental puzzle that was consuming him. He had to go back to the Pizzaplex and check out the game again. He had to test out his theory.

Because Miles and his dad and sister had come back early from their camping trip—something about Miles falling into a bed of poison ivy—Archer was occupied for the evening. He'd gone over to his friend's house to play Monopoly, an attempt to distract Miles from "all the itching." Kane didn't have to worry about Sienna, either. She was annoyed enough with Kane to want a "solo sloth evening" instead of a date. He was free to head back to the Pizzaplex to do a little recon on the food-fight machine.

Feeling a little silly walking into the Pizzaplex arcade on his own, Kane did his best to stroll nonchalantly, as if he was just a cool senior with a little time to kill. Kane wasn't obsessed with his image like some of the other jocks he knew, but he didn't want to look like a friendless nerd—although that thought felt really disloyal to

Archer. How could he love his brother and judge nerds at the same time?

Because of the AI within.

When Kane ducked into the Fazcade Tag-Team player cave, the rest of the arcade's sounds diminished just a little. He hadn't noticed that last night. But then, last night he hadn't been on a mission to figure something out, a mission that made him wish he could get some silence so he could focus and think.

Only three of the game's orange chairs were occupied, so Kane was able to sit on the end. Not only was it important he sat somewhere else to test his hypothesis, but he was happy for the bit of distance from the three other players; one of them, or maybe all of them, didn't smell so good. The smell was a cross between dirty socks and sweat. These were odors Kane was pretty used to—his team's locker room wasn't exactly an olfactory paradise— but that didn't mean he liked them. He started breathing through his mouth as he settled himself in his chair.

Inserting tokens into the machine, Kane leaned forward and studied the control panel. The night before, Archer, who was an arcade game whiz, had called up their personas for the game. Kane had to concentrate to pick Orville again. He wanted to be the same player so he could try to re-create some of the things he'd observed the night before.

Kane managed to choose Orville, but as the orange elephant popped into view on the curved screen, Kane suddenly realized he'd have no control over what partner he got. What if—

He needn't have worried. Montgomery Gator walked up next to Orville and held out a black-clawed hand for a high five.

Kane, trying not to be too freaked out by Monty's obvious recognition of Kane, aka Orville, used the joystick so Orville could return the high five.

Kane looked up at the golden circle above his head. It was bright again, the same way it had been during the game the night before.

"Okay," Kane muttered. "Let's see what happens."

For the next ten minutes, Kane blocked out everything except the food fight playing out on the screen in front of him. While at once doing his best to avoid getting bombarded by food and attempting to score points with well-aimed attacks of his own (peaches and plums were his ammo of choice tonight), Kane carefully observed Monty's behavior in relation to Kane's strategy and Orville's resulting moves. As had happened the night before, Monty tended to freeze up whenever Kane was overanalyzing, and Monty was in the flow when Kane was.

Kane took his hand off the joystick and looked up. The circle of light above his head was flickering just a little. If Kane hadn't been looking for the slight variations in brightness, he didn't think he would have seen them. But they were there. The light was linked to something that was in turn linked to the game . . . and very probably to Kane.

But how did it work? Kane had to know.

Kane jumped to his feet. He looked up at the light, which was still blinking. Were the movements coordinated with Kane's brain waves, as he suspected? And how had Fazbear synced up to his mind?

Kane climbed onto the orange vinyl chair and touched the circle of light. What had looked like just a glow of light from below was clearly a circular heavy plastic panel. It was covering whatever was the source of the light.

Kane tightened his grip on the panel and attempted to shift it. When gently shoving the panel didn't do more than wiggle it, he clamped his teeth together the way he did when he was concentrating on catching a long ball trying to clear the fence, made a fist, and pounded on the cover.

Sparks shot down from the edges of the plastic like a meteor shower. Kane ducked his head as he heard sizzles around him, and the food-fight game screen went dark. So did all the lights in the game.

Even though the Fazcade Tag-Team game was mostly in its own cave, plenty of light spilled in from the rest of the dazzling arcade. Kane, therefore, was able to clearly see all three little boys in the other vinyl seats look up at him and scowl.

"Hey!" the spiky-haired kid said. "What'd you do?!"

One of the other kids, a blond boy with long hair that flopped over pale blue eyes, pointed at Kane. "He broke the game!" the boy yelled.

"Yeah," the third kid, who had hair even yellower than his floppy-haired buddy, chimed in. The gap between his front teeth was obvious when he pulled back his lips and shouted, as he pointed at Kane, "It was him! He did it!"

Chagrined, Kane jumped off the vinyl seat. He wasn't going to find out anything else tonight. He turned to leave the arcade.

As Kane approached the game cave's entrance, with the boys still shouting accusations behind him, the curly brown-haired attendant stepped around the corner of one of the pinball machines. She looked past Kane and saw the darkened screen. Then she shifted her attention to the boys, who were still pointing and screaming at Kane.

The girl frowned at Kane and pressed her lips together.

Before she could say anything to him, though, he gave her a short nod and strode away from the food-fight game. Tucking his chin, the same way he did after he missed a catch in a game, he kept his eyes on the arcade's bright red carpet as he got out of there as quickly as he could.

Kane returned home from the Pizzaplex just before his mom got home from work. The phone rang as they both walked into the kitchen.

His mom picked up the phone from the white marble counter near the stainless-steel fridge. Kane, still preoccupied with the arcade, didn't pay attention to what his mom was saying until she put down the phone and turned toward him.

"Archer is staying over at Miles's house," she said. "Apparently, Archer is doing a good job of distracting Miles from his misery." She dropped her massive taupe purse onto the kitchen island and plunked herself down on one of its dusty-blue plush stools.

Kane took the stool next to his mom's. He noticed that the pale yellow linen pantsuit she'd put on that morning was just as fresh and unwrinkled now, twelve hours later, as it had been then. She looked just as perky, too. How did she do that?

Kane ran a hand through his hair, which felt limp. That was how he felt, too. He couldn't seem to shake off what had happened at the arcade.

Kane's mom stood and went to the fridge. Pulling out a bottled protein drink, she opened it and took a big swig as she turned back to Kane. "I assume you and Sienna went out? You ate?"

Kane shook his head. "Yes," he said.

Liar, liar, pants on fire.

He blinked. Where in the heck had that come from? He'd never called himself that before. He'd also never thought in that taunting tone. And besides, he wasn't lying. He'd answered the question about eating, and he had eaten. He'd stopped by the Corner Deli and grabbed a turkey sandwich on his way home from the Pizzaplex.

But you didn't go on a date, he thought. *Half lie, half lie, half lie.*

Kane frowned. Reacting to his teasing self-talk, he clarified. "I mean, yes, I ate. But no, Sienna and I didn't go out. She wanted a sloth evening."

Kane's mom smiled. "I could use one of those," his mom said after she swallowed more of her drink. "But I guess I'll settle for a long bath."

She looked at Kane. "Are you okay? You look a little"—she frowned and studied him—"stressed, I guess. You have some tightness under your eyes there."

Kane shook his head. "I'm okay. Just thinking about all the stuff I need to get done."

You're full of it, he thought.

Rattled and tired, Kane stood and prepared to tell his mom that he was going to turn in early. Instead, he heard himself saying, "I'm going out for a run."

"Okay, hon," his mom said. "Be careful. Be sure you wear that reflective vest." She smiled at him when he rolled his eyes. Then she finished her protein drink and tossed the bottle in the trash. "I'm going to turn in after my bath. I'll see you in the morning." Kane's mom stood on her tiptoes. He leaned down for a peck on the cheek.

When his mom walked out of the room, Kane didn't move. He wasn't sure what to do next.

He didn't want to go for a run. Why had he said he was going to go for a run?

Run, run, run, he thought. For a strange second, Kane felt like doing a little jitterbug step. Then the urge passed. He walked out of the kitchen and started toward the stairs leading up to the second floor of the house.

Because interior design was his mom's business, her own home had to look "magazine-spread-worthy," or so she said. As a result, Kane was used to living in a house that was filled with design trends that "popped." The almost-black-stained walnut floors, the gray-silk-wallpapered walls, the chrome accents in a living room filled with linen-covered plush furniture, and the modern art and sculptures strategically placed throughout the main living area were not what he'd call comfy and inviting. But apparently, they were "chic."

Party time, Kane thought as he bounded up the stairs.

Kane noticed the way he was moving and wondered why he was doing it. He also had the sudden desire to grab one of the framed modern art prints from the wall and throw it down into the foyer.

What was wrong with him?

Kane suppressed the bizarre destructive urge. He bolted into his bedroom, where his mom's interior design efforts did not intrude, and he shut the door.

Looking at the room that was as familiar to him as his own skin, Kane thought, for the first time ever, *What's with all the gray in here?*

"I like gray," Kane said out loud.

Kane walked to his queen-size bed and flopped down on it. Stretching out, he gazed around his room.

Lots of gray, he thought as his gaze circled the large room. *Boring!* The word stretched out in his head—*boooorring.*

"I like gray," Kane repeated as if reassuring himself.

He liked black, too. Black and silver were the colors of his favorite major league baseball team.

Admittedly, Kane had been Archer's age when he'd picked out the gray paint for his walls, along with his black-painted shaker-style headboard and matching dresser, nightstand, chest of drawers, and metal credenza-style desk. At the time, he'd also picked posters of his favorite baseball players for his walls. He'd since outgrown those and replaced them with a couple framed sketches of baseball diamonds and even more framed photos of Sienna, his friends, and Archer. Most of the room was like a pictorial of his high school years.

Boooorring, Kane thought again.

Kane screwed up his face and rubbed his temples. What was boring? Why did he think that?

Unlike a lot of kids, Kane had enjoyed high school. Sure, it helped that he was one of the sports stars in his class. But he liked learning, too. It had been his idea, for instance, to tackle the subject of his essay. His friends had all picked sports topics, but Kane had thought the workings of the left and right brain were really fascinating, and he'd been happy to do the research.

Fascinating like a wart, Kane thought.

"Okay, that's enough!" Kane snapped. He sat up and grabbed his head.

What was going on with him? It was like someone else was thinking the thoughts in his head.

Kane shot to his feet and ran to the bathroom. He stared into the oval mirror above his gray—yes, gray—rectangular sink. He looked at himself in the mirror.

Other than the fact that his carefully created blowout hairstyle had gone limp sometime during the evening at the arcade, Kane looked the same as he always had. Didn't he?

Kane leaned toward the mirror. He squinted at himself. As he did, he saw the tightness under his eyes that his mom had mentioned. He also saw something else, a kind of smart-aleck glint in his eye, as if he was looking back at himself with condescending—and critical—amusement.

While Kane was gazing into the brown eyes that for some reason had a bit more gold in them than he remembered, he suddenly winked at himself. The wink sent him stumbling back from the sink.

"I did not just wink at myself," Kane said out loud. His words seemed to bounce off the bathroom's gray-travertine-tiled walls and come back at him.

Yep, you did, Kane thought.

"I'm just tired," Kane said to himself.

Yeah, that's it, sport, he thought. *Lie, lie, lie.*

Kane clamped his hands over his ears. Shaking his head, he grabbed his toothbrush from its black holder by the sink.

Waah, waah. Baby needs to go beddy-bye, he thought as he vigorously brushed his teeth.

Kane did his best to blank out his mind as he finished with his teeth and headed to his bed. When he again thought, *run, run, run*, he started listing major league baseball players and their stats in his head. After just a couple dozen of them, he drifted off to sleep.

The next day was a Friday, and Kane was happy about that. Getting through the school day had been brutal. The bizarre thoughts wouldn't stop popping into his head. It seemed like everything he saw triggered some new judgment that he'd never made before. He felt like he was losing his mind.

Although he hadn't felt like himself all day, it wasn't until the end of his date with Sienna that he'd faced what was going on with him.

After grabbing a chicken burrito at a new stand at the weekend farmers market, Kane and Sienna had strolled through the market hand in hand, as they often did. The market was like an upscale, grown-up version of the Pizzaplex's arcade. Nearly everyone who came to the market was in a good mood. Happy chatter and laughter and dozens of mouthwatering food aromas were a backdrop for checking out displays of local produce, artisan foods, and nearly every art and craft you could think of.

Kane didn't enjoy "poking around" all the displays as much as Sienna did, but he loved being with Sienna, so he never complained about their farmers market dates. And when Sienna spotted something that she liked, generally something really inexpensive, he'd buy it for her. She loved that.

"You're so romantic," she'd told him hundreds of times.

Tonight, Sienna was a little off. She had a pimple on the end of her nose, and she was self-conscious about it. "It was there when I woke up this morning," she'd said to him when he'd picked her up before school. "Don't look at it."

Can't take my eyes off it, he'd thought, chuckling inwardly. *It's bigger than Chica's cupcake!*

Shocked not only by the unkind thought but also by a comparison to a Fazbear character, Kane had wisely said, "It's not noticeable. And even if it was, your beauty trumps it."

Sienna had smiled and given Kane a kiss as he had listened to a long snort in his head. *Fast and loose*, he'd thought. *What a line.*

Kane had frowned. It wasn't a line. He really thought Sienna was beautiful. And what did "fast and loose" mean anyway?

"Hey, look at these!" Sienna said now, tugging on Kane's arm. She led him toward a kiosk that sold miniature animals made out of seashells. "Oh, they're so clever," she said as she scanned the shelves. She flashed a smile at the elderly woman who sat on a black canvas director's chair near the stuff she had for sale. The thin gray-haired lady smiled back at Sienna and winked at Kane.

Sienna plucked one of the little shell animals off its shelf. "It's a sloth!" she squealed, clearly delighted.

Kane glanced at the sign that listed the prices of the animals. The little sloth was only six dollars. He could buy that for her.

Kane started to reach for the sloth. Before his hand got to it, though, for some reason, he turned. His gaze landed on a kiosk that sold natural skin products. MADE FROM HONEY AND OATS AND A LOT OF LOVE, the kiosk's sign read.

Kane, wanting very much to take the sloth from Sienna's hand and buy it, instead nudged Sienna and pointed at the skin-care kiosk. "You should put back that sloth," he said. "Let's go over there, and I'll buy you something for the big zit on your nose."

I'm the man! Kane thought. He had a strong urge to grin and do a fist pump. *I'm a hoot*, he told himself.

But what he'd said wasn't funny. It was childish and mean. Why had he said it?

Sienna, her face flushed and her eyes narrowed into slits, put her back to Kane. Without saying a word to him, she pulled out some money and bought herself the sloth. Then she thanked the old lady and marched away from the kiosk without even glancing at Kane.

"That was a bonehead move, young man," the old woman said.

Kane heard a roar in his head. *Sticks and stones*, he thought.

And that was when he realized he had to accept the truth.

But not now. First, he had to make up with Sienna.

Kane took off after Sienna. He had to practically run to catch up with her because she was striding quickly through the farmers market.

"Sienna," he called out. "I'm sorry. I don't know what got into me."

But the thing was that he did know. He absolutely knew.

Unfortunately, though, there was just no way he was going to be able to explain it to her. It was too incredible.

"Get away from me!" Sienna flung at Kane when he came up beside her and tried to take her arm. She shook off his hand.

"I'm really sorry," Kane tried again.

"Forget it," Sienna said. "You're right. My zit is huge. So, I think I'll just take my zit home and spend the evening with it. It's massive, but it's a lot nicer than you are."

Sienna broke into a trot and started jogging away from Kane. He followed her.

"Let me drive you home," he called.

"I'd rather get a ride with a serial killer," she shouted.

Several couples turned and looked at Sienna. She ignored them.

The couples were looking at Kane, too. He might as

well have had a neon sign over his head that read STUPID BOYFRIEND.

Not stupid, Kane growled in his head. *What would have been stupid was buying the dumb sloth. The skin cream thing was rock and roll!*

At this point, even if he could have convinced Sienna to get in his car with him, Kane wouldn't have driven her home. He couldn't be with her right now. He was too mind-blown.

Or actually, he was mind-possessed.

That was what was going on, he understood now. It had happened at the Pizzaplex, in the food-fight game cave.

Like any normal human, Kane had a voice in his head. He'd had one for as long as he could remember. The voice chattered at him about what he needed to do, how he could do better, and how he should have done that and shouldn't have done the other thing. The voice made projections about the future. It worried and fretted. It also schemed and complained. It compared, and it assessed. Kane's voice, like all inner voices, was a very busy voice. It rarely shut up. The voice, the left-brain aspect of Kane that had motivated him to learn about the way the brain worked, was Kane's AI computer self. And Kane was used to the voice. He knew how to use it for his own good, and he knew how to ignore it when necessary. He also was familiar with the tone of his inner voice. He knew what *he* sounded like in his head.

So Kane knew that he was hearing a new voice in his head. *His* voice was still there, some of the time. But another voice had joined it.

Kane knew who that new voice belonged to.

As strange as it sounded, Kane was sure that the

new voice in his head belonged to Montgomery Gator. Monty's AI, via the food-fight game at the Pizzeria, had somehow gotten into Kane's neurocircuitry when they were playing the game. And it wasn't leaving. Monty was now a resident in Kane's head. He just hoped he wouldn't be a permanent one.

All the strange thoughts Kane had been having since the night before, all the snarky little judgments that had been running through his mind—these weren't his own. The thoughts sounded just like things Monty had said in the game. Obviously, the thoughts belonged to Monty.

It had been Monty who had suggested skin cream instead of a sloth made of shells.

Crocs eat sloths for snacks, Kane thought.

"Shut up," he muttered.

And he groaned. How was he going to live with not one but two AI voices in his head?

Somehow, even as he wrestled with what was happening to him, Kane managed to get to sleep that night. He also managed to haul himself out of bed the next morning, have breakfast with his mom, and hang out with Archer after Archer got home from Miles's house. Kane even got to the school in time to catch the team bus to Saturday afternoon's game. Several times during the ride he'd tried to call Sienna, but she wasn't taking his calls. He didn't blame her. But he kept trying.

After he and his teammates trooped aboard the old team bus, which belched the sharp odor of diesel fuel as its engine surged and the bus jolted into motion, Kane took out his phone yet again. He tapped Sienna's number on his screen.

Leaning against the bus's cool window and turning a

little to try for some privacy, Kane waited for Sienna to answer. But she didn't.

So what? Kane thought after he'd left his tenth message and wondered if he still had a girlfriend. *Who needs a girlfriend?*

"I do!" Kane said loudly.

"Yeah, well, I didn't propose, dude," Kane's buddy Lewis said.

Kane elbowed Lewis and tried to look relaxed. "I'd accept Frank's proposal before I'd accept yours," Kane said, gesturing at their burly bus driver

Frank glanced over his shoulder. "I ain't asking, either," Frank called out.

Kane laughed. His laugh, however, was more than a little strained.

Kane *had* to stop arguing with himself. Whatever Monty said in Kane's head, Kane needed to keep his mouth closed. He succeeded for the remainder of the bus ride.

Once the game began, luckily, Kane's thoughts were only on the game. There was no room for Monty in Kane's concentration.

By the top of the ninth inning, Kane had scored four runs. Unfortunately, his teammates weren't doing as well, and the other team was up by one.

Kane came up to bat with two outs. It was up to him. If he didn't get a hit, they'd lose.

As he always did when he was preparing to take the plate, Kane took a deep breath to block out the fan noise— both the jeers and the yells of encouragement. He couldn't split his attention between what he had to do and what he was hearing. As part of his pre-batting ritual, Kane took seven, exactly seven, practice swings on deck, and then he went through his routine at the plate. He scuffed one foot in the dirt and then the other. Dust wafted up around his ankles. He waggled his bat. He tapped home plate with the end of the bat twice. Then he faced the pitcher.

The other team's pitcher was a short guy, but he had power. He also had an evil knuckleball.

Knuckleballs were rare pitches, especially in high school baseball, and the pitchers who used them tended to use them almost exclusively. This guy, though, a beaky-nosed guy with heavy freckles and dark, almost black eyes, only used the knuckleball sporadically. Mostly, he brought the heat, which was good because Kane could power through fastballs.

Kane, however, missed the pitcher's first two fastballs. He thought they were outside the strike zone. The ump, who emphatically called both pitches strikes, disagreed.

When Kane squared up to bat after his two strikes, the afternoon's breeze carried the smell of hot dogs and popcorn and the scent of the freshly mowed grass from the outfield across the plate. On the heels of the aromas, Kane looked into the pitcher's eyes, and he knew, without a doubt, that the guy was going to throw a knuckleball.

Because Kane liked being a well-rounded hitter, he had spent hundreds of hours hitting knuckleballs. He knew how to adjust his stance to have a better chance at connecting with the erratic pitches that tended to dive just as they crossed the plate. So, now, because he just *knew* the guy was going to throw a knuckleball, Kane shifted his feet and the position of his arms.

Stop that, Kane thought. *Widen your stance. Get ready to rock and roll. He's going to throw heat.*

He is not, Kane argued with himself.

Actually, he was arguing with Monty.

Kane raised a hand and stepped out of the batter's box. "Sorry," he said to the ump.

The ump straightened. He gave Kane a hard look.

Kane turned away from the ump and muttered under his breath, "Not now." He couldn't have a face-off with the gator AI while he was at bat.

A fastball's coming, Kane's inner-Monty thought. *And fastballs are fun to hit.*

Kane knew Monty was wrong about what the pitcher was going to throw, and who cared what kind of pitch was more fun to hit. Kane needed to make contact with the ball, fun or not. He had to set up for a knuckleball. In spite of this intention, when Kane stepped back into position at the plate, his arms and legs moved into the fastball-ready position. He didn't want them in that position, but that's where they went.

He only throws one or two knuckleballs a game, Monty thought. *He's already thrown three. No way is he throwing a dumb old knuckleball.*

But that's what the pitcher was going to throw. Kane knew it. He could feel it.

Unfortunately, he was right.

Being right didn't do him any good, though, because his arms and legs had refused to prepare for a knuckleball. They'd been ready for a fastball; so of course the knuckleball got past him.

"Strrr-ike three!" the umpire shouted with an over-exaggerated fist jab aimed in Kane's direction.

The other team erupted from their dugout. The home fans cheered.

Angry and frightened by his inability to make his body do what he'd wanted it to do, Kane threw his bat and stomped away from the plate. "Told you so," he muttered as he retrieved his bat and jogged, with his head down, toward the dugout.

Before Monty had commandeered Kane's arms and legs at the baseball game, the only thing Monty had done besides intrude into Kane's thoughts was make Kane suggest a cream for Sienna's pimple. Kane, of course, was nearly unglued by the realization that he had an AI gator in his head, but he'd rationalized that Monty's thoughts and the occasional insertion of those thoughts into Kane's speech wasn't the total end of the world. It was bad, yes. Very, very bad. And Kane didn't know what he was going to do about it. But he figured he could handle it. For the most part, even though Monty was in his head, *Kane* was the dominant presence in his mind.

After the game, however, Kane had to come to grips with the terror of knowing Monty could take over his body at will.

Kane sure as heck couldn't tell anyone about it. The reception his essay had gotten had been bad enough. If he started talking about an animatronic AI in his head, he'd be instituted for sure.

He just had to hope that Monty would remain content with a back-seat position.

On Monday, at lunch, Kane was distracted as he stepped up to the buffet line in the school cafeteria. It was hard not to be distracted when you shared your thoughts with a mischievous gator. Some things he could do without concentration, though, and picking out what he was going to eat was one of those things.

The cafeteria was already packed when Kane took his

place in line because he'd gotten hung up in the restroom after class. In the restroom, Kane had done his thing and was at the sink washing his hands when Gerald, the class nerd, had walked in.

It would be fun to stick his head in the toilet, Kane had thought when he saw Gerald.

As soon as he'd had the thought, Kane had shaken his head. He'd pressed his lips together and concentrated on lathering his hands.

"Hi, Kane," Gerald said.

Kane hadn't trusted himself to open his mouth. Having a nerd for a little brother, Kane had nothing against Gerald, and because other kids were mean to the poor guy, Kane went out of his way to be nice to him.

Monty, however, had other ideas. *Where'd he get that nose?* Kane (Monty) thought. *It looks like someone glued a potato to his face.*

Used to Kane's friendliness, Gerald had frowned when Kane didn't speak. Kane had tried a smile, but as he started to stretch his lips into a grin, his tongue attempted to poke its way out.

Kane immediately clenched his teeth so his tongue couldn't escape. Monty was trying to stick Kane's tongue out at Gerald!

"Did you see the meteor shower last night?" Gerald asked, hovering near the sinks.

A couple sophomores came in. Arguing about a movie they'd just seen, they ignored Kane and Gerald.

Is that how this little guy got to earth? Kane thought. *He rode down on a meteor?*

Kane heard roaring laughter in his head. Frowning, he managed to nod in answer to Gerald's question.

By now, Kane had finished washing his hands. He'd started to pull his hands out from under the water, but his hands didn't want to come. They were trying to cup water as if they intended to throw water on Gerald.

"Cut it out!" Kane snapped.

Gerald's already bulgy eyes expanded even farther. His face started to screw up like he was going to cry.

"Not you," Kane managed to say over the top of the thought, *Crybaby! Crybaby!*

"I was talking to myself," Kane said. This was true, in a way.

Lie, lie, lie, Kane thought.

"Sorry," Kane said as he'd started to hurry past Gerald. "I have, uh, a lot on my mind."

Not daring to look at Gerald again, Kane had torn out of the restroom. Once through the door, he had leaned back against the wall. Ignoring the looks he'd gotten from two giggling freshmen girls, he'd run a hand through his hair and muttered, "Get a grip."

Kane lifted a hand to wave at his teammates, who were settled around their usual table in the cafeteria. Kane moved his tray along the line. Inhaling the jumbled smells of chili, hot dogs, spinach, and spaghetti, he thought, *Now, there's some great ammo for a food fight!*

"Don't even think about it," Kane mumbled.

Thankfully, even though Kane was only a couple feet from the brown-haired junior girl in front of him and the two freshmen boys behind him, the rumble of conversation, the clinks and clunks of plates and cutlery, and the pulsing pop music coming from overhead speakers drowned out his comment. Thinking he had himself under control, Kane started to choose a green salad from the food on the cafeteria buffet.

When Kane almost had his right hand on the large plate of greens, the hand veered away from the greens and grabbed a bowl of cherry Jell-O. As soon as he grabbed the Jell-O, Kane let it go. The bowl dropped back to the bed of ice it had sat on. Kane attempted to go for the green salad again, but his right hand headed back toward the Jell-O.

Frowning, Kane lifted his left hand and got the salad he wanted. At the same time, his right hand grabbed the Jell-O.

Kane put the green salad on his tray, and he tried to get his right hand to put down the Jell-O. His hand wouldn't cooperate.

Because Kane didn't want the Jell-O, he managed to prevent his hand from putting it on his tray, but he couldn't stop it when his right hand suddenly lifted the bowl and flung the Jell-O into his face.

Stunned, Kane immediately looked around to see if anyone had seen what had happened. Unfortunately, three girls at the table closest to the food line had seen it. All three widened their eyes at him, but none of them spoke. Kane recognized the girls. They were sophomores. One of them had a brother on the baseball team, and all three of them came to the games. So, they knew who he was.

There was a hierarchy in high school, and Kane was at the top of it. Even when he did something weird, kids on the lower rungs of the ladder weren't going to call him on it.

Ya think? he thought. *What if you do this?*

Before he could get himself under control, Kane's right hand flipped the green salad up from his tray, flinging lettuce all over his shirt. As the lettuce scattered, Kane's right hand reached for a bowl of macaroni salad. Even though he tried to grab the salad with his left hand, Kane's right hand managed to lift the bowl and upturn the salad onto the top of his head.

Kane could hear riotous laughter in his head. *Points for me!* he thought.

Kane tried to get a hold of his right wrist with his left hand, but he was too fast for himself. His right hand evaded his left, and he found himself lurching down the food line, shoving his tray along the stainless-steel shelf as he went. Before he could stop himself, Kane picked up the ladle that rested in a big pot of chili. The ladle, filled with chili, lifted upward. The spicy scents of jalapeños and chili powder assaulted Kane's nostrils.

Kane squinted at his right hand, and he shot out his left hand to grip the ladle's handle. For several seconds, his right and left hands fought over the ladle. Chili squirted onto his tray and shirt and splashed onto the floor.

"Just what do you think you're doing, young man?" a woman's shrill voice cried out.

Kane looked up from the ladle. His gaze landed on the small, intense eyes of one of the cafeteria workers, Mrs. Patel, a dark-haired woman with severe frown lines and thin lips. Mrs. Patel stood behind the food in front of Kane. Her hairnet cut into the flesh of her forehead, making her skin bulge above her scrunched-up brows.

Kane dropped the ladle. Chili slopped over a pan of tamales next to the chili pot.

I win! his thoughts chortled.

Kane looked at Mrs. Patel. "I'm really sorry, Mrs. Patel. I'll clean up the mess."

Kane glanced around. The three girls weren't the only ones staring at him now. Dozens of pairs of eyes were directed his way, including those of his teammates and those of Sienna and her friends, who were sitting at the table near Kane's teammates.

Kane—his face sticky with Jell-O, his shirt covered with lettuce and chili stains, and his hair gooey with macaroni salad—threw up his hands and gave everyone his best cocky grin. "Sorry, everyone," he called out. "Social experiment. An assignment. Go on back to what you were doing."

Gimme five, Kane thought. *Good one.*

Kane blocked out his thoughts as he grabbed a bunch of napkins. He started to bend over to clean up the mess he'd made.

"Leave it," Mrs. Patel said. "I'll get it." She shook her head and muttered, "Strange teachers. Social experiment, my patootie."

"Thanks, Mrs. Patel," Kane said as he deposited his tray in the dirty dishes area.

What about eats? he thought. *I'm hungry.*

"Tough," he muttered as he turned and strode out of the cafeteria. No way was he going to risk another one-man food fight.

At practice that afternoon, Kane took some good-natured ribbing about his "social experiment." Fighting urges to hawk loogies and kick dirt at his friends (*ah, come on, let's have some fun*), Kane managed to keep up the charade that he'd been throwing around food to see what people would do.

"What was the point of the experiment?" Tank, the team's right fielder, asked. He rolled up his sleeves over bulging biceps before he took a few practice swings.

"To see if I could start a food fight by tossing around a little food," Kane said, thinking fast.

"At yourself?" Lewis asked. He was warming up nearby, firing fast balls at Jimmy, the team's catcher. "That's pretty tame, if you ask me."

Kane shrugged. "Yeah. I didn't get to do what I wanted to do."

Before the conversation could continue, Kane started doing wind sprints. He had to get away from his friends because he hadn't been the one speaking just then. Monty was the one who'd said he didn't get to do what he wanted to do. Monty had wanted a full-on food fight.

You're no fun at all, Kane (Monty) thought.

And in the middle of the second wind sprint, Kane did a somersault. Not because he wanted to.

From that point on, Kane had to concentrate on every move he made. Rigid focus was the only way to keep Monty under control.

That afternoon after practice, Kane went to the school's shop so he could finish up his project. Because Sienna still wasn't talking to him, he wanted to complete what he was working on so he could give it to her and hopefully get her to forgive him. He also wanted to do something to get his mind off what was happening to him.

When Kane pushed through the double doors to the school's woodshop, he found it empty. That was fine with him. He was still embarrassed by what he (Monty) had done in the cafeteria. And overall, it was getting harder and harder to interact with other people because Monty kept butting in, usually just with snide judgments in Kane's head but sometimes forcing Kane to blurt out things he didn't want to say. So far, none of those things were as bad as what he'd said to Sienna, but he had gotten his share of raised brows and rolled eyes.

Kane let the metal doors fall closed behind him as he strode past the massive self-feeding table saw. By far the biggest tool in the place, the saw had twelve feet of spinning metal rollers that carried long pieces of wood to the saw's blade to be ripped lengthwise. A sheet of plywood lay on the roller. Kane could tell by its sweet, almost wintergreen-like scent that it was birch. He idly wondered who'd left it there.

The shop room was shaped like an inverted T. The horizontal part of the upside-down T extending both ways from the doors contained the shop's large power tools—the radial arm saws, band saws, table saws, table routers, drill presses, and planers. Behind these tools, the vertical part of the T contained the worktables. The shop's walls were lined with storage shelves and cabinets. Some of the cabinets were used to store students' ongoing projects. The rest were packed full of tools and woodworking supplies; the shop was stocked with every hand tool imaginable, a vast array of clamps, shelf after shelf of glues and stains and paints, and all shapes and sizes of nails, screws, and other connectors.

When Kane had first signed up for shop class, he and his fellow "newbies" had been told that the shop was the finest school shop in the country because a rich alum had gifted the school with all the amazing tools it contained. Kane hadn't realized just how necessary all these tools were at the time, but he'd come to realize how lucky he was to learn woodworking in this shop.

Kane reached the worktable he usually used, and he

retrieved his partly completed project from the cabinet behind it, ran a hand over the cutting board, and appreciated the smooth feel of the perfectly sanded wood.

Looking good, Kane thought. He wasn't sure if that thought was his or Monty's. He had found that they did sometimes agree on things.

Kane was making a cutting board for Sienna, who lately was really interested in cooking. He'd already done a lot of the work. He'd painstakingly cut pine strips, glued them together, and sanded them smooth. Kane planned to cut the glued-together pieces into a sloth shape, making it probably the world's only hanging-sloth cutting board.

Grabbing a cordless jigsaw, Kane positioned the saw's thin blade at the middle of the sloth's rounded back, and he gripped the saw's handle with his right hand. Kane moved his thumb, intending to start the saw. Before he could depress the switch, however, he picked up the saw and moved it to the outer edge of the glued-together boards.

Then Kane's thumb turned on the saw. The saw started cutting zigzags along the edge of the boards, but that wasn't what Kane wanted. He wanted to start his cut next to the template. So, he tried to move the saw to the right place.

The saw wouldn't move. It wouldn't move because his hand wouldn't make it move.

Sloths are boring, he thought. *A sun would be more fun.*

"Oh, no, you don't," Kane said.

The jigsaw, rhythmically humming away, was continuing to buzz along the edge of the wood, making little triangles. Kane gritted his teeth and used every ounce of his will and strength to jerk the saw inward, away from the edge and toward his template. As soon as he moved the saw in that direction, though, it started to pull back toward the edge again.

"Stop it!" Kane snapped. He put his left hand over his right hand, and he bore down, struggling to get the saw to stay near the template.

But the saw jerked backward again.

Kane tugged, and the saw veered toward the template once more.

Its blade still powering up and down, the saw began to career all over the surface of the glued-together boards. Kane grunted and struggled to control the saw, but he ended up overcorrecting, and the saw powered right through the middle of the sloth template.

Kane and Monty were locked in a battle over the cutting board, and neither of them were winning. But the big loser? The big loser was the cutting board.

Kane could do nothing but continue to fight to gain control of his body while he watched all the work he'd done get chewed to pieces by the jigsaw. Since neither of his hands could master the jigsaw, it seemed to develop a mind of its own, and it just carved up the wood at random.

He had to turn the saw off.

He had to wrestle with his own hand to do it, but Kane finally was able to turn off the saw. When it went silent, he set it down and stared at the pile of wood shards and sawdust that was supposed to have been Sienna's sloth cutting board.

★ ★ ★

The next morning, Kane woke up twenty minutes before his alarm was set to go off. This was very weird. But no weirder than sharing brain space with an animatronic gator.

Get out of bed, sleepy head! the now all-too-familiar inner voice singsonged in Kane's head. *Let's rock and roll!*

Kane groaned. He put his pillow over his face.

Party pooper, he thought.

Kane threw the pillow across the room.

Fighting despondency, Kane reached out and picked up his phone from his nightstand. He sat up, put his feet on the floor, and called Sienna. As he had the previous fifty times he'd called over the last few days, he got her voicemail.

"Listen, Sienna," Kane said into his phone, "I wish I could explain to you what's going on with me. Because something is going on. I have—oh, I don't know how to say it—I've been saying things I don't mean. And I"—Kane managed to get his thumb on the red end-call button on his phone just in time, as his mouth finished— "think you're stuck-up for getting so bent out of shape about one little comment about your huge zit."

Forget her. Let's have some fun, Kane thought. No. Not Kane. Monty.

Oh, come on, Kane thought. *Get in the game. Offering to buy her cream for her big zit was funny.*

But that wasn't what Kane really thought. Or was it? Kane was starting to wonder which thoughts were his and which were Monty's. What would happen if Monty took over even more?

Disgusted and discouraged, Kane stood and headed into the bathroom. He didn't know what else to do except try to stick to his regular routine. It was either that or give up and possibly turn into Monty. Plus, part of him was holding out the hope that if he kept trying to ignore the Monty part of his brain, the AI would get frustrated and crash or something.

Kane took his shower, got out, and wrapped a towel around his waist. He stepped over to his sink. Ignoring his wet hair, he reached into the drawer in the cabinet under the sink. There, he kept his hair products, his razor, and his scissors. He grabbed his razor and quickly shaved. Then he started to reach for his blow-dryer. His right hand froze before he could grab it.

A blowout is girly, he thought. *A mohawk would be more fun.*

Before he could stop it, Kane's right hand went back into the drawer and grabbed his razor again. Kane immediately knocked the razor from his right hand with his left hand.

"Not the hair," Kane said.

He looked at himself in the mirror. Squinting, he leaned forward.

"I know you're in there," he said. "But you're not in command. I am."

Against his will, Kane leaned toward the mirror. The right side of his mouth quirked up into a snotty grin.

You're in trouble now, he thought.

Kane's right hand shot into the drawer and grabbed the razor again. It lifted the razor, and it moved the razor toward the side of his head. The razor was almost touching Kane's hair when his left hand reached up and slapped the razor away.

The razor rocketed across the bathroom and hit the

travertine tile near the shower with a tinkle. It hit the floor—*tappity-tap*—and spun in a circle.

Kane again tried to pick up his blow-dryer. And again, his right hand wouldn't cooperate. He rolled his eyes and grabbed the blow-dryer with his left hand.

Thinking he'd won the hair battle, Kane didn't realize what his right hand was doing until a pair of scissors appeared in his field of vision. The scissors opened and headed toward the long waves of hair on top of his head.

"Hey!" Kane shouted. He dropped the blow-dryer and lifted his left hand to grab the scissors.

As Kane's left hand attempted to wrest the scissors from his right hand, his right hand turned the scissors. It slashed one blade of the open scissors across Kane's left palm, ultimately driving the point into the meaty part of the palm under Kane's thumb.

Kane gasped and yanked his left hand back. The scissors stuck in his flesh for a second, then dropped away and clattered into the sink. Blood poured from the gash in his palm.

Kane didn't make it to school that day until after lunch. He spent the entire morning in the ER, waiting to get his hand stitched up.

Surprisingly, though, the afternoon passed uneventfully. For nearly four hours, all through the rest of the day's classes and through baseball practice (Kane had insisted on practicing, even though using his left hand hurt like heck), Kane hadn't heard a peep out of Monty. Kane's thoughts were finally his own. His words were his own. His actions were his own.

Maybe something about the injury had thrown Monty out, Kane thought as he cleaned up after practice. And that was his *own* thought.

He'd never been so relieved.

After practice, Kane started to head toward his car. His hand was throbbing, and all he wanted to do was go home, lie down, and forget the last few days.

So why was he walking down the hallway in the opposite direction from the parking lot?

Kane was so distracted by the pain in his hand and the euphoria of thinking his problem was over that he was halfway down the beige-tiled, locker-lined hallway before he realized that his feet were taking him some-place his consciousness had no intention of going. As soon as he caught on to what was happening, Kane tried to stop his feet.

But his feet kept going.

"What are you doing?" Kane asked aloud.

One of the artsy kids in his class, Rowen, whose kohl-lined eyes made him resemble a zombie, was standing at his locker. He turned and leveled his hollow-looking gaze at Kane.

"What's it to you?" Rowen challenged.

Kane wanted to explain that he hadn't been talk-ing to Rowen, but his mouth wouldn't open. His feet kept moving, and he walked past Rowen without saying a word.

Rowen shrugged as Kane went by. "Whatever," Rowen muttered.

When Kane thought he was out of Rowen's earshot, he whispered, "What are you doing?"

He was talking to Monty because clearly Monty was

the one moving Kane's feet. Monty wasn't gone after all. Monty was the one taking Kane to . . .

. . . the school's shop.

Kane pushed open the double doors to the shop. It was empty.

"Why are we here?" Kane asked, moving forward without any desire to do so.

Monty remained silent.

Kane turned and walked toward the self-feeding table saw. Frowning, he reached the end of it, and he levered himself up so he was seated on the plywood that still lay on the metal rollers.

"What are you doing?" Kane heard the panic that tinged his words.

Kane concentrated and tried to push himself off the plywood. Instead of lifting him up and away from the saw, one of his hands gripped the plywood and the other one reached out and flipped the switch to power on the saw.

A high-pitched whine filled the room, and the saw blade buzzed into motion. The metallic screeching roar filled Kane's head.

The saw's sound, though, wasn't loud enough to silence Kane's—no, Monty's—thoughts: *I've tried to play along with you, but you're no fun. You need to go away.*

"What do you mean?!" Kane shouted.

Concentrating on regaining control of his muscles, Kane grunted with the strain of attempting to push himself off the flat expanse of birch. But again, his body did the opposite of what he wanted. He lay back on the plywood.

As soon as Kane was in the prone position, the plywood started to move along the metal rollers. Kane, able to control his head just enough to crane his neck to the left, looked back at the saw's huge spinning blade. The saw's shrill keen filled his head as his heart began to pound as fast as the saw was whirling.

"Stop!" Kane screamed.

The plywood kept moving toward the saw. It carried Kane with it.

"No!" Kane screeched as his head moved closer and closer to the saw blade.

Kane strained to keep his gaze on the whirring metal, jagged-edged disk. He could see that the saw was positioned so it would cut through the center of his head if he couldn't get control of his body and get off the plywood. If he remained where he was, the saw blade would slice right through the crown and bisect his skull, severing his corpus callosum.

The saw's going to cut my brain apart, Kane thought. *And the rest of me, too.*

Kane felt the blade cut into his skin. He howled as the saw buzzed relentlessly, preparing to carve into Kane's skull. His thoughts a chaos of pain and horror, Kane could do nothing to save himself.

The table shook violently as the saw struck bone. *Rock and roll!*

BLEEDING
HEART

HER NAME WAS DAISY ZAYLAND.

She was the coolest girl in Bayer High School.

To Danny Shullenberg, anyway.

And she was walking straight toward him.

Well, walking down the school hallway where he happened to be standing by his locker.

When she walked, her blondish-brown hair swayed at her shoulders. Her eyelashes fluttered over her golden eyes. Her eyebrows were perfectly arched. Her face was heart-shaped. He knew because he'd sketched her a bunch of times. Not that she knew anything about that. Daisy never gave him the time of day.

She was super cool and he was, well, average.

He often considered himself a neutral shade on the color spectrum. Something you blended with other colors to make them lighter or darker. Something usually overlooked and unseen.

Not Daisy.

She was like a vibrant purple or a dazzling orange. A color that caught your eye right away and didn't have to mix with another shade because she wasn't meant to blend in. She was meant to shine and be unique.

When he sketched her, he even drew the little star she had tattooed on her wrist. Yes, Daisy was the only girl at Bayer High who had a *real* tattoo. Not one of those stick-ons that only lasted a couple of weeks. A real one outlined in red that was permanent. He wanted to ask her how she managed to get it. Or if she had any more? How had she convinced her parents to agree since she was still in high school? But he never got up the nerve to ask or even talk to her.

Danny thought she was going to walk right past him like she usually did, but she actually stopped right in front of him. She smiled and flashed her perfect teeth.

He swallowed hard.

He felt a little tingle in his heart.

Suddenly, something tiny flew at him and hit his nose. *A dumb bug, probably.* So mesmerized by Daisy, he brushed it away.

"Hi," she said. Her voice was soft, yet confident.

He waved a nervous hand and blushed. Oh wow, he

was such a dweeb. He looked down at his worn tennis shoes doodled with black ink, cleared his throat, and met her eyes. "Um, I mean, hi."

Something else hit his forehead. He slapped it away. He couldn't believe *Daisy Zayland* was actually speaking to him. This was the greatest day of his life.

"Danny?" she said.

Wow, she actually knew his name. "Yeah, Daisy?"

She tossed her hair over her shoulder with her hand, placed a hand on her hip. "Your breakfast is ready."

Danny blinked. "Huh?" Another something—was it a bug?—hit his cheek and fell to the ground. Then another. Danny glanced down at the floor. Fruity cereal circles were scattered around him.

Wait . . . what was happening?

He looked at Daisy once more.

She frowned at him. "I said, *Danny, your breakfast is ready.*"

Danny blinked awake on his twin-sized bed in his room. He spotted his M. C. Escher poster of two hands drawing each other on the wall, and the stacks of graphic novels on his bookshelves.

He was definitely at home. Not at school.

Of course, it had been a dream. Daisy Zayland had never graced him with her attention in real life.

But it had been such a nice dream.

"Danny, I said, your breakfast is ready," his mom called out from somewhere in the house. "Hurry so you're not late for school, 'kay! Bobby, rise and shine!"

Another fruity circle hit his face.

Danny sat up, rubbed at his sleepy eyes, and spotted his

three-and-a-half-year-old little brother, Johnny, stand-ing in the doorway of his bedroom with a plastic cup full of cereal in his hand. He was gleefully taking aim and launching his breakfast loops at Danny's head.

"Hey! Stop that, Johnny!" Danny scowled at him.

Johnny giggled and threw a handful that showered his carpet and bed like confetti, then stuck his tongue out and ran away.

Little monster.

Danny sighed, shoved back his covers, and placed his legs over the side of the bed. He stretched his arms out and yawned.

His mother filled his doorway next. Her brown hair was pulled back away from her full cheeks. She wore her pastel-green dental assistant scrubs.

"Danny, I've been calling you. Get up, kiddo. Your toaster tarts are on the table." She looked down at his carpeted floor. "For goodness sake, Danny, what is this mess?! You're cleaning this right up! I don't have time for this!" She huffed as she rushed down the hallway. "Bobby, get up. Come on now! You have enough tardy slips to fill my purse. Let's go!"

"I'm awake, Ma," Bobby called out.

Danny's shoulders sagged in quiet frustration before gathering the fruit circles from his blankets and then slid off his bed and onto the floor. He picked up the rest of the fruity cereal and tossed them in his little trash can by his desk. He straightened and walked out of his bed-room scratching his head, down the hallway, and into the kitchen. There were his toaster tarts on the table at his seat. He didn't even like toaster tarts anymore, not since the fifth grade, but his mom didn't listen to him so he ate them anyway. There was fresh fruit and eggs on a plate for Bobby since he was in training mode with his workouts. Although Danny wasn't sure what Bobby was ever training for. It appeared to Danny that his older brother was always lifting weights and flexing his muscles in the mirror for his own enjoyment.

Danny, on the other hand, was on the thinner side, with skinny arms and legs. He'd never been into sports, and his mom always told him that when he was little he spent most of his time daydreaming by himself and coloring in coloring books, instead of playing with Bobby or any school friends.

Some things didn't really change, he guessed.

Danny grabbed a toaster tart and walked into the front room to study their Christmas tree. It was a real Douglas fir tree, sitting crookedly in the stand in front of the window. Years of handmade ornaments were hung on the branches, and tangled lights were wound around it. Tinsel was thrown all over by Johnny's crazy, decorative hand. Dad hadn't seen it yet. He was still traveling with his job and would likely be home right before the holiday in a couple of weeks.

"'Oo-'ooo!"

Danny nibbled on his tart and turned to see his little brother on his big brother's shoulders, raising his arms and shouting, "'Oo-'ooo! 'Aster, 'aster!"

Bobby held on to Johnny's legs and speed-walked through the living room. "Speed mode!" Bobby rushed past Danny, moved around the coffee table, and then launched Johnny onto the big, cushiony couch, then proceeded to tickle him in his neck.

Johnny burst out laughing. "'Nanas! 'Nanas!"

Bananas was the family code word for surrender.

Johnny had started speech classes a month ago and was working with a therapist to pronounce all his sounds when he spoke. But everyone in the family had learned to understand him just fine. Just not anyone outside of the house.

Both of Danny's brothers got their dad's honey-blond hair and Danny inherited his mom's dark brown. Which was fine, Danny supposed. He didn't need to be exactly like them, anyway.

Mom rushed into the front room with Johnny's jacket and lunch box. "Boys, that's enough! I'll be home at five. I expect you guys to get started on your homework before I get home so you're not up late getting it done. Keep an eye on Johnny till I get home. He'll be dropped off at four after speech therapy."

"I got something after school, Ma," Bobby told her. "That school meeting I told you about. It's for college applications, remember?"

She sighed. "Right, right. That leaves you, Danny. Be home by three thirty. 'kay?"

Danny nodded. Not that Mom looked over at him. She always seemed to be on a fast-forward setting. Rushing around taking care of the house, working full-time, while dad was away for his job, and taking care of three boys. Even at fifteen, Danny accepted that it was a lot. So while his little brother was a can-do-no-wrong little monster and his older brother talked a bunch and monopolized his mother's attention, Danny had grown to be the quiet one. The one who didn't cause problems. He really only enjoyed drawing in his sketchbook and keeping to himself, anyway.

★ ★ ★

All cleaned up and dressed for school, Danny hooked on his pale blue backpack. He'd decorated the front pocket with drawings of trees and animals with black marker. He grabbed his graphite pencil and hooked it over his ear and headed out the front door to walk to BHS. His older brother brushed past him.

"Out of the way, Danny boy!" Bobby's friend, Tyler, was picking him up in his beat-up old truck, which had two rusted fenders and tires that had seen better days.

Danny watched his older brother hop into the passenger seat and slam the heavy door shut. Music blasted as they took off from the curb. A spurt of white smoke puffed out of the old muffler.

Danny turned around and locked the front door, then took off for the two blocks to his school. The winter morning had a harsh chill. There was a thin layer of ice on car windows and rooftops. The town of Marston didn't normally get snow, maybe twice in the last fifty years as locals often shared, but this winter was especially frigid. Danny and his brothers often wished it would snow for the holidays.

When Danny hit the first corner, he spotted his best friend, Aaron Glasgow, waiting for him. Aaron's backpack was hooked on his shoulders, and he held his flute case in his right hand. He wore dark, rimmed glasses that looked strange over his long nose. The glasses were secured with a band that wrapped around his head and kept his glasses secured so he wouldn't lose them during school activities. He wore pressed khakis and a knitted red sweater and scarf that his mom likely made for him. Danny and Aaron had gravitated toward each other in preschool since they were the only ones who would sit in one place for hours instead of running around chasing each other on the playground like the other kids.

"Hey," Aaron said to him.

"Hey," Danny said back, as they continued on to school.

"Did you read the latest *Blake, the Hero* graphic novel?"

Blake, the Hero was about an average high schooler named Blake Billings, who didn't have a lot of friends. But he had a secret persona, Hero, who wore a bright red mask and helped right wrongs in his small town just by using his smarts.

That was why Aaron and Danny liked it so much. They could relate to being a nobody like Blake, but they dreamed of being a cool, secret, teen superhero like him. And, of course, Danny liked all the illustrations. He might want to be a graphic novelist one day.

"Is it out already?" Danny asked Aaron.

"Yeah, yesterday. I made Claudia drive me over to the mall and wait in line to get it." Claudia was Aaron's older sister.

"Oh wow, do you think they sold out, already?"

"Don't know. But maybe we can go after school?

Danny began to nod, then remembered Johnny. "Can't. I have to be home when Johnny's dropped off later."

"Oh, well, do you want me to tell you about it?"

Danny held up a hand. "No way! I hate spoilers."

"Okay, but it's super good. I stayed up late and finished it. How about the latest *Ouno Samurais* issue?"

Danny shook his head. He'd been a little distracted lately, he guessed.

"You are *way* behind."

The boys walked up to the entrance to Bayer High as other kids swarmed in. The hall was loud with voices. The walls were covered with bright posters for school events and activities that Danny always ignored. He wasn't much of a joiner. They finally squeezed through groups of kids and made their way to Danny's locker to exchange books for first period.

"You got to get the latest copies right away," Aaron told him. "I need someone to talk about the novels with *really bad*."

"I'll try," Danny said, then he looked around and pulled out the latest drawing he'd made of Daisy from his backpack.

"Hey, what is that?" Aaron asked, then said flatly, "Oh, another one."

It was a character-style illustration of Daisy Zayland as if she was in a graphic novel. Danny quickly walked across the hallway, a few lockers down to Daisy's, slipped the drawing through the vent, and went quickly back to his locker to stand by Aaron.

His breaths thinned because he was a little nervous about Daisy catching him.

"How long are you going to be sneaking her drawings?" Aaron asked. "Why don't you just talk to her?"

Danny shook his head as his cheeks warmed. "No, I can't. She's too . . ."

"Stuck up?"

"No!" Danny shook his head, pulled the pencil from his ear, and rolled it between his thumb and fingers. "Just way cooler than me, that's all."

Suddenly, Danny felt that little tingle in his heart and

quickly turned toward the front entrance. Sure enough, he spotted Daisy maneuvering through kids down the hallway by herself, and it was like rock music played in his head as she moved. He wondered if he was the only one who felt like that when he saw her. Even though Daisy was really pretty, she didn't seem to have a lot of friends. Other girls tended to stare at her from a distance in awe because she had a tattoo and they seemed to begrudge her for being different. But Daisy always looked confident and didn't seem to worry what other kids thought of her.

"Gosh, it's like you have a sixth sense with her," Aaron told him. "So weird."

Maybe he did. That had to mean something, right?

Danny watched her walk past him with a tote bag hooked over her shoulder and a binder hugged against her. Today she wore a pretty purple sweater, a puffy black jacket, faded blue jeans, and black boots. Her hair was wavy and brushed back behind her shoulders.

"Hi, Daisy," Aaron said, out of the blue.

Danny's eyes widened as he nervously glanced at his best friend, who must have gone completely bonkers. *They never talked to Daisy Zayland.*

Daisy turned her gaze to Aaron and then actually turned her eyes toward Danny for a millisecond.

Oh, wow.

Daisy Zayland actually *looked* at him and met his eyes. For the very first time.

It was like something clicked within him.

He felt his entire body temperature rise.

Daisy shifted her gaze toward Aaron and lifted her eyebrows, seemingly uncertain, then gave a half wave as she glided by.

Danny spun around and shoved his best friend's shoulder. "Are you crazy?!"

Aaron snickered. "You should have seen your face! I thought you were going to pass out! That was so classic!" He laughed so hard, he started to cough so he pulled out his inhaler from his pant pocket and took a puff into his mouth, sucking in the meds.

"Do you really know Daisy Zayland?" Danny asked his best friend.

Aaron slipped his inhaler back into his pocket. "Why do you say her full name like that? *Daisy Zayland is so pretty. Daisy Zayland, I love her.*"

"*Shhhhhhh!*" Danny quickly glanced over his shoulder. "Quiet."

"I have Geometry with *Daisy Zayland*. No big deal."

Danny's eyes widened. "You never told me!"

"You never asked." Aaron shrugged. "It's not like we talk to each other. She's *way cooler*, remember?"

"You are seriously lucky. What's she like?" Danny prodded. "Is she good at math? She's probably really good at everything."

Aaron frowned. "Nah. Sorry, not much to tell. She's just a regular girl. Kinda snobby if you ask me."

Danny slowly shook his head. "No way. She's the prettiest girl at Bayer." He remembered the first day he'd seen her at Bayer High. It was his second day of ninth grade. He was struggling with his locker combination. He happened to turn around and lean back against his locker, defeated. And there she was walking by like a breath of fresh air. Everyone seemed to be staring at Daisy because there was just something about her that made you look. Danny had stood mesmerized by her as his stomach hitched. When she was finally gone, Danny turned around to open his locker and miraculously it opened!

Right there and then, he knew Daisy was special.

Aaron stared at him, shaking his head. "You got problems, Danny. Got to get to class. See you at lunch." Aaron took off and disappeared into the mass of kids.

Danny waited another moment as Daisy opened her locker. He held his breath when she spotted the drawing. She reached in to grab it and glanced at it, then looked around the hallway.

Danny whirled away and turned to look inside his own locker, his heart beating erratically. "Stay calm," he murmured. *Would she love it?* he wondered. *Would she take it home and pin it to her wall? Or maybe tape it to the inside of her locker?* Pride filled him like a balloon at the thought.

He waited a moment, took a breath, then turned to look back at her over his shoulder. But she was gone.

He looked around but couldn't find her. All that he saw were a bunch of moving kids he hardly knew.

Huh. She could have slipped the drawing into her binder to take it home, he thought, *or left it in her locker for the time being.*

Danny shut his locker and started to walk to his first period. He spotted a crumbled-up piece of paper on the floor by her locker.

Frowning, he picked it up.

As he unwrinkled it, his heart sank.

It was the drawing he'd made for her.

Daisy Zayland had discarded his artwork like a piece of garbage.

★ ★ ★

That evening, Danny sat at the dinner table with his mom and two brothers. It was chicken strips and mashed potatoes night. Dad's seat was empty as usual, but Danny couldn't wait till he got home for Christmas. His dad was the greatest. He wasn't home a lot because he had to travel to teach other companies how to use new corporate computer software, and the boys knew it was a good-paying job in order to support the family, but it didn't stop them from missing him.

When Dad came home, he was real patient with Danny and his brothers. He'd listen to all their stories and then he'd spend time with each of them while he was home for a few days. He was really supportive of Danny's art, always telling him how good his work was and how he could find a good job as a digital illustrator one day.

Danny couldn't wait to talk to his dad, man to man. He had something new to discuss with him beside art. And it had to do with how to impress a girl.

He wanted to ask his dad how he got his mom to like him. He just knew his dad would give him the right advice. After all, his parents were high school sweethearts.

Mom got up to clear her plate and strolled into the kitchen when her cell phone rang at her seat. Danny's eyes widened, as he was sitting next to his mom's chair and could see who was calling on the screen.

"Who is it?" Bobby asked him from across the table.

Danny didn't answer him, because he knew his brother would try to grab the phone first. Danny snatched the phone and stood up to answer it. "Hi, Dad."

"Heya, Danny. How you doing, son?"

Danny smiled hearing his dad's cheerful voice. "Good. Everything's good."

"Let me talk to him!" Bobby snapped as he stood up and rounded the table.

Danny maneuvered in the other direction.

"'Addie? I wanna 'alk to 'addie," Johnny cried out from his chair.

"Hey, Dad, when you get home, I need to tal—*hey!*"

Bobby grabbed the phone out of his hand like a rotten thief!

"Hi, Dad! How's it going?" Bobby said into the phone. "Yeah? That's good. You wouldn't believe the grade I got on my recent Econ test. Blew it out of the park."

Danny pulled at his older brother's muscular arm, but he was too strong and tall. Bobby shoved Danny away, with a palm to his face. Danny fell to the carpet, annoyed.

Johnny was next to Bobby, hopping up and down, trying to reach for the phone. "'Addy! I wanna 'alk!"

Mom came barreling out of the kitchen. Her cheeks were rosy and her eyes were bright whenever Dad called. "Boys! Stop that! Bobby, give me the phone, please."

"Okay, Dad, here's Mom. Love you!" He handed the phone to Mom.

"Hi, honey, yes, just finished up dinner. How was your day?" Mom strolled into the kitchen for some privacy.

Danny was on his feet, pointing a thumb to his chest. "I got the phone first, Bobby, and you know the rules." Whoever got the phone first was supposed to be able to talk to dad for a minute. After all, Bobby had made the dumb rule himself.

Bobby shrugged his big shoulders. "Yeah, well, you cheated. You wouldn't say who was calling."

"Whatever. You just want to hog Dad to yourself all the time."

Bobby shook his head and made a circle with his finger toward Danny's face. "Watch out, Danny boy. You're turning a little green."

"Yeah, well, you may be older, but sometimes you act like a baby." Danny stomped over and grabbed his plate from the table to take it to the kitchen.

"'Ot 'air," Johnny whined. "I wanna 'alk to 'ad."

Both of my brothers are so annoying, Danny thought.

That Sunday, after a load of Christmas shopping, Mom surprised Danny and his brothers with a stop at Freddy Fazbear's Mega Pizzaplex for a late dinner. The boys all hooted with joy when Mom pulled into the busy parking lot.

"Cool, Mom, thanks!" Bobby told her.

"'Ega 'izza!" Johnny shouted, with his arms waving in the air.

"Yeah, thanks, Mom!" Danny told her.

"You're welcome, boys. A little treat for you guys. Sorry, I'm so busy lately." There it was—that little crack in Mom's voice when she started missing Dad. "Come on, let's go have some fun."

Danny gazed about as they entered the large entertainment establishment while bright lights flashed in every direction, from fun and fast rides to neon-lit posters featuring the amazing features of the Pizzaplex—Monty's Gator Golf, Fazer Blast, Roxy's Raceway, the Fazcade, gift shops, and more! Music and game pings and bells overpowered Danny's senses. He smelled pepperoni pizza and something sweet and syrupy. Crowds of families swarmed the first floor, holding their little kids' hands or trying to run after them. It was chaotic entertainment in every direction and Danny and his brothers loved it!

This time, bright Christmas decorations caught his eye. Danny had never seen the Pizzaplex during the holidays before. There were several decorated trees in every entertainment section of the massive building. Shiny ornaments and wreaths hung on the walls with several twinkling lights.

"Whoa," Danny whispered. He gazed to the upper floors, seeing the handrails glowing with lights and adorned with Christmas wreaths. He nearly ran into Glamrock Freddy as the character waved to everyone while wearing a Santa hat. Danny shifted past him, gazing at the shiny lightning bolt on his chest. All the Pizzaplex workers were dressed as elves, wearing red vests and red hats with fake pointy ears. It was so funny and cool!

Bobby ran ahead and found them an empty table in the far corner of the eatery. Families had their tables filled with pizza, soda, paper plates, and napkins. Mom ordered them a family-size pepperoni pizza.

After their fill of pizza and soda, his mom gave Danny and Bobby a handful of tokens while she took Johnny to the little kids' area to play.

"Let's meet at the entrance in a half hour, boys," she told them. "Have fun and watch out for each other."

Bobby and Danny took off to the Fazcade where they quickly started playing arcade games. It wasn't long after that Danny used up all his tokens and got stuck watching his brother play an arcade game. Bobby was always way better at the games than Danny.

Danny observed a boy and girl holding hands as they

walked around the games, and he thought of Daisy. He really wished he could talk to his dad about her. He looked up at his older brother. Bobby's blond hair was unruly and nearly in his eyes. His cheeks were pink because it was warm in the arcade with all the kids. Danny remembered Bobby having a short-term girlfriend during his freshman year. It had only lasted a week, but maybe he could give Danny some girl advice . . .

"Bobby, can I ask you a serious question?" Danny asked, squinting up at him.

Bobby rolled the circular ball embedded on the arcade game panel and with his other hand slapped at the three buttons in order for his player to evade animatronics.

"Bobby?" Danny said, "can I ask you a serious question?"

"What, Danny? Can't you see I'm playing here? Aw, dang it! Look what you made me do? I lost the game! I was so close to getting the top score."

"Never mind." Danny started to walk away.

Bobby sighed. "Okay, okay. What's the question?"

Danny turned back to his brother, who was now leaning against the arcade game he'd just lost on, his arms crossed. He wore his usual outfit of sweats and a hoodie.

"Well, it's about . . ."

"A girl," he said flatly.

Danny's eyes widened. "How did you know?"

Bobby shook his head like his brother just didn't get something. "Hard to miss you always drawing her in your sketchbook all the time." Bobby grinned. "Her name's a flower, right? Rose or lily or whatever?"

"Daisy." Danny narrowed his eyes. "Have you been spying on me?"

"Get real, I have way better things to do. What's the

matter? You want to kiss her or something?" He proceeded to pucker his lips and make annoying kissing sounds that made Danny's face heat.

A girl walked by and gave Bobby a weird look. Bobby cleared his throat and straightened.

"No! Just forget it!" Danny flung out his arms in frustration. How could he think his brother would ever be serious? He whirled around to stomp off, when Bobby hooked a hand into his hoodie bringing him to a halt and spun him around.

"Hold up. I'm just playing around. What do you want to know, then?"

Danny crossed his arms, then huffed out a breath. "Well, I just wanted to know how you get a girl to talk to you?"

"Talk?" He scrunched up his face and waved a hand toward Danny. "That's easy. You just go up and ask her a question. Then introduce yourself. Not that hard."

Maybe it wasn't hard for Bobby, but for Danny it wasn't so easy. "Well, then how do you get a girl to even notice you?"

Bobby rubbed at his jaw and studied Danny's face. "You really like this girl?"

Danny nodded. "Yeah, but she's way more interesting than me."

Bobby shook his head. "You got to be more confident, Danny, come on. You want to know what girls like?"

Wide-eyed, Danny nodded.

"Presents," he said, with certainty. "Give the girl a nice gift and you're instantly on their radar."

Danny tilted his head. "A gift?" His dad did bring his mom flowers every so often.

"Oh yeah, something she's interested in. Some of them like cutesy stuff, like a stuffed teddy bear. Maybe a bracelet, candy, or something artsy. Depends on the girl, though."

"Well, she didn't like my drawings very much."

Bobby shrugged his shoulders. "Maybe she's not into art."

Danny's spirit took another hit at the reminder. "She likes art. Just not mine."

"Why? What'd she say when you gave her your drawings?"

Danny shifted uncomfortably on his feet. "Well, I didn't, actually, talk to her."

Bobby rolled his eyes. "*Come on.* You have to talk to the girl, Danny. It's kind of required when you like someone and you want them to like you back." Bobby looked around and spotted something across from the arcade. "Hey, look over there."

Danny swiveled his head in the direction his brother pointed. There was a Santa's Giftplex area that had opened up for the holidays.

"Find something in there and give it to her. But you gotta introduce yourself this time when you do." Bobby gave him a big shove in the back and Danny stumbled forward. "Go on. I'll let Mom know you're shopping for a gift for a friend."

"*Hello, families, the Mega Pizzaplex will be closing in fifteen minutes!*" the loud speaker announced.

"Oh no," Danny murmured as he rushed over to the Giftplex. He didn't have that much time to pick a special gift for Daisy. He pulled out a five-dollar bill from his pocket. He also didn't have much money to buy a nice gift, either.

Danny speed-walked into Santa's Giftplex and instantly became mesmerized with the surroundings. Bells were jingling to holiday songs. Roxanne Wolf stood at the entrance, waving to everyone who walked in and out. The animatronic wore a Santa hat and had white fur on the edges of her red outfit.

Everywhere Danny looked he saw bright red and green decorations with hints of winter flakes and frosted glass. There were special booths spread out in the great room. Some were lined with stuffed dolls and action figures of Glamrock Freddy, Glamrock Chica, Montgomery Gator, and Roxanne Wolf. Chocolate candies and cakes were displayed that looked too perfect to eat. Christmas lights hung from the ceiling and little trees were placed all along the walls. There was a poster booth and a T-shirt and sweatshirt booth, all with the Mega Pizzaplex logo. Purses and backpacks were hung in one area; in another, there were cups, posters, plastic toys of all different colors, and magical balls with funny characters in them. Gifts recommended for your mom and dad, such as candles, books, scarves, and socks were in a different place.

"Whoa," Danny whispered, wide-eyed. This was one of the coolest gift shops he'd ever seen. He spotted a few kids surrounding a booth in the far corner. Curious, Danny walked over to get a closer look.

The sign above was written in neon letters: GIFT WRAP-PING. A large window of frosted glass stood as a barrier while a present was being decorated with wrapping paper and tied with big, frilly bows set upon a glass table as if by magic! There wasn't an elf or a helper involved at all and no one was holding the present.

Wow.

The colorful designs on the wrapping paper spread across the paper with special ink that seemed to flow like water. The bows were spiraling and spinning like twirling dancers. The gift was set on a glass table and the paper was magically wrapping the box by itself and being sliced away to fit the gift perfectly.

But how?

"How is this happening?" Danny asked, in awe.

A kid next to him answered, "I don't know but it's the coolest thing I've ever seen. I just keep buying small things and sticking them in the little door just to watch it get wrapped by itself."

Danny nodded in agreement. He finally noticed the mini door in the glass where the presents could be placed inside.

He heard a girl shout over to his right, "Wow, this is so funny! Hahaha! It tickles so bad!"

Next to the gift wrapping booth, behind the same frosted glass, a girl had her arms inserted into two holes in the glass that connected to a large, iron vat that was secured behind the frosted barrier. The outside of the structure was painted bright red and wrapped with glowing lights. It was shaped liked something he'd seen in a history class—an iron lung, which is a long, narrow device that could hold a person's body to help them breathe or something.

Danny tilted his head, wondering what was happening to the kid. Then the red lights surrounding the iron lung flashed to green and the girl pulled her arms out to reveal that her arms were painted with colorful tattoos!

"It's just like I imagined!" she shouted. "Oh my gosh,

I love them! Don't you love them?" Her friend gasped and admired the new artwork. The tattoos were bright with colorful designs of butterflies and flowers.

Danny's eyes widened in excitement as he instantly thought of Daisy Zayland. *She would love something like this! But how* was *it working?* he wondered. *What kind of magic was being used to paint the wrapping paper and draw on the kids' arms?*

He had to know!

If he could somehow impress Daisy Zayland with this unique body art, it would be truly awesome!

"Five minutes, families. Please finish up your activities and slowly make your way to the exit!"

Danny's excitement deflated as he was running out of time. He swiveled his head around as kids started walking out of Santa's Giftplex.

He blinked as a quick idea formed. He took his cell phone out of his back pocket and texted his brother:

Tell mom I'm running late in the bathroom. Stomachache. Please wait for me. I'll try and hurry.

Bobby: Mom said hurry up. We'll be in the car.

Danny smiled. He looked around and when he watched Roxanne Wolf turn away, he ducked behind a fake Christmas tree beside the frosted glass of the magic gift wrapping booth. He sat on the red carpet and pulled his knees to his chest as his pulse drummed. He looked through the frosted glass as another box was being magically gift wrapped.

A few minutes later, the lights in Santa's Giftplex

dimmed. He peered around the tree and didn't see any more employees lurking around. Maybe he could somehow find an opening to the booth. The small door to put in the presents seemed too compact and too high to get through. He curiously pushed his palms against the glass and realized it was some kind of thick plastic that could bend! *He could actually slip inside!* He pushed harder and squeezed his body through the gap, falling onto the cement floor littered with scraps of wrapping paper and clips of ribbon.

His three slices of pepperoni pizza felt like a rock in the pit of his stomach. He was so nervous!

Above him, he watched through the clear glass table as a gift continued to be wrapped. He eagerly inched closer.

He squinted his eyes and discovered something tiny was moving with the wrapping paper. Something *really* minuscule, and there were a lot of them!

He moved even closer under the table as his eyes adjusted to the quick movement.

He gasped. It wasn't magic at all—but the littlest robots he'd ever seen!

The bots had to be the size of a grain of rice. They seemed to fly through the air and they had no feet. They appeared to be the color of the frosted glass, so that was why it was hard to see them from far away. He couldn't see their hands as they moved in a blur of motion, working quickly to wrap, color, and draw.

These little bots were amazing!

Fascinated, he watched them do their incredible job for another moment when he felt his cell phone vibrate with a text. Likely Bobby telling him to hurry up.

The tiny bots were magical, all right. They seemed to create instantly with unlimited capacity. If he had his own bots, he could be tattooed with different designs every single day. And it would be his own little secret.

He would have something really cool in common with Daisy Zayland.

She would have to notice him for sure!

Nearby, he heard keys rattling with footsteps. His pulse sped up. It had to be a security guard checking to see if everyone was cleared out! Uncertain, he whipped out his hand and tried to grab a couple of the bots. But he missed them! They moved really fast.

He narrowed his eyes as he jerked out his hand again and was able to grab a couple into his palm. He quickly stuffed them into his front pocket and squeezed back through the plastic window.

Oh wow, oh wow, he murmured in his head. He felt like his heart might race out of his chest. He just hoped he didn't get caught.

Danny crawled from behind the tree to the back of another booth until the coast was clear. He ran to the front entrance and out the door. His breaths were rushing from his mouth.

In the parking lot, he spotted his mom flashing the car lights and honking the horn. He ran over, opened the door, and jumped into the back seat.

"You okay, hun? Too much pizza?" his mom asked him.

He swallowed hard, and licked his dry lips. "Yeah, um, I'm okay, now." He felt a little sting on his thigh and lightly tapped the bots in his pocket to settle them down.

We'll be home soon, he thought.

"Boys, I completely forgot we're low on milk," Mom said. "Making a quick stop at the store before heading home."

From the front passenger seat, Bobby looked over at Danny's hands to see if he'd gotten a gift for Daisy. When he noticed his hands empty, he shook his head in what looked like disapproval.

But Danny wasn't empty-handed at all.

He had the best gift in his pocket that would literally change his life.

When they finally arrived home after picking up more than just milk at the store, Danny rushed to his bedroom, closed the door, and locked it. He slid his hand into his pocket and felt for the bots.

A spurt of shock rippled through his body.

His pocket was empty!

No, no, no!

He stuffed his hands in both pockets and pulled out the pocket linings. His five dollar bill floated to the floor.

No bots!

Crushed, he fell onto the bed, arms spread out.

He'd lost them! They'd must have fallen out somewhere. He hadn't been prepared for his spontaneous heist so, of course, it hadn't worked out. Why hadn't he been more careful?

There went his fantasy of Daisy Zayland really noticing him for a change.

After a few more moments of self-pity, he sighed and accepted his defeat. Probably for the best, anyway, he decided. His parents always taught him and his brothers to do the right thing, and stealing was wrong. He heard his mom yelling for everyone to get ready for bed, so he got up to do just that.

Maybe he'd actually get up the nerve to talk to Daisy Zayland one day . . .

Yeah, right.

Aaron: Have to stay in class @ lunch. Make up test. See U after school.

Danny read the text from Aaron at the beginning of lunch. *Great, now I have no one to sit with*, he thought. Normally, he didn't mind being alone, but he hated sitting by himself in high school. It felt like everyone stared and made fun of you if you were by yourself. First, he'd lost the bots, and now he had to be a loner at lunch. Just great. He decided he'd do some drawing in his sketchbook in the school library where everyone had to be quiet, anyway, and he didn't mind being spotted alone.

He walked in and scanned around for an empty seat at a table. The library was filled with wall-to-wall shelves lined with books. In the center were various worktables and a computer station. There were a few kids already scattered about the area, reading books or doing homework.

At a far corner table, he spotted Daisy Zayland!

Instantly, he felt that funny tingle in his heart. She was sitting alone, turning pages in a large book. He grabbed the graphite pencil from his ear and nervously rolled it between his fingers.

He could find another seat far away from her . . .

Or he could take a chance, like his brother had said, and actually talk to her.

He wasn't sure how long he stood there, trying to debate with himself. When he finally murmured under his breath, "Just do it already."

Swallowing hard, he walked across the library. It felt like it took forever. Kids gawked at him, giving him strange looks.

He wondered why. Did he have a funny look on his face or something? Did he forget to comb his hair? Did he have a new zit?

He finally got to the table and stood there awkwardly, uncertain of what to say as he tapped the pencil into the palm of his left hand.

Daisy turned a page in the book and Danny realized she was looking at a tattoo book.

He slipped the graphite pencil back onto his ear. "Hi."

She glanced up with an uninterested look on her face and looked back down at her book. "Hi," she answered.

Go on, say something else!

Like what?

He stared and stared until it finally dawned on him—the tattoo book! He was such a dweeb.

"Um," he said, "what tattoo do you like best?"

She looked up and blinked at him.

"Um, in the book," he babbled. "Are you thinking of getting another one? I mean, I saw the little star you have on your wrist—which is fantastic by the way—and I figured you were wanting to get another one, which is understandable. Um, yeah."

Stop rambling!

She twisted her lips, and Danny thought she might

ignore him when she finally pointed to a small, simple heart at the bottom of the page. Her fingernails were painted purple, he realized.

"I think this will be my next one. Maybe on my side." She pointed to above her hip.

A rush of joy came over Danny. Daisy Zayland was talking with him! *Yes, yes, yes!*

He tried not to smile too big. "Yeah, that would be really cool. I mean, that's what I want, too."

Suddenly, a sharp pain dug into his side. He slapped a hand there. *Ow.*

Daisy looked up at him, her eyes direct as she scanned his face. It was like she was really seeing him for the first time.

"You like tatts?" she asked.

He nodded.

"What's your name?" she asked.

"I'm Danny."

"Daisy."

Perspiration lined his head as the pain in his side increased. *What's happening?* "Yeah, I know."

"Do I have a class with you or something?"

"Um, no. I—" Another sharp pain drilled into his side so suddenly that he abruptly keeled over with a yelp. He heard kids make *Shhhh* sounds and the librarian said, "Quiet, please."

"Hey, what's the matter?" Daisy asked, her expression suddenly concerned.

"Uh—nothing. I gotta go."

Danny whirled around and noticed the kids were all staring at him again. Embarrassed and unsure what was happening, he sprinted out of the library, holding his stinging side. Breathing hard, he rushed into the boys' bathroom and into a stall. He ignored the scent of old pipes and stinky water and dropped his backpack on the floor. He pushed aside his zip-up sweatshirt and lifted his T-shirt. He was shocked to see a couple of lines of blood dripping from above his hip. Bewildered, he blinked. "What happened?"

Danny grabbed some toilet paper and dabbed at the blood. Something was *cut* into his skin, he discovered. He lowered his head to try and see what it was but was unsure what to make of it. He pushed out of the stall and stretched up on the tips of his toes to get a better view in the mirror.

His eyes widened in disbelief. "How the heck did that happen?"

Carved into his skin, about the size of a quarter, was a small heart.

The bots, Danny thought as he hurried to his locker. It had to be the bots. There was no other way for a heart to be suddenly engraved into his skin. But there was supposed to be a drawing *on* his skin, not a carving *into* his skin.

He thought he'd lost the bots last night.

What the heck was going on?

He had no idea!

He spun the combo on his locker and opened the door.

"Hey, there you are."

Oh wow, that was Daisy's voice!

Danny whirled around to face her. He was breathing hard. "Oh hey, Daisy," he said, and waved nervously with his hand.

"What happened? Why'd you take off so fast in the

library?" She glanced down to his side and noticed some of the blood on his T-shirt. "Ouch. Did you hurt yourself or something?"

He nervously grabbed for the pencil in his ear and realized it was gone. He must have lost it. "Um, it's nothing. Really. Just a scratch."

"Should you go to the nurse?"

Danny stepped back. "*No.* I mean, not right now. I gotta get to class."

"What's the matter with you?" She frowned at him. "You're acting really weird."

Danny froze. He didn't want her to think he was weird, but he didn't know if he should show her, either! Gosh, he could really use a girl handbook right about now. Reluctantly, he shifted his sweatshirt aside and lifted his shirt to reveal the little heart carved in his skin. This was so embarrassing!

Daisy stared at his side for what seemed like eternity. "What? How?" Then her lips curved. "That is really . . . *cool.*"

Danny's jaw dropped open. "Really?" He blinked a couple times. "I mean, you like it?"

"Yeah, I'm super impressed by your skill. The lines are clean. The heart is perfect. And you did it so fast . . ." She met his eyes and it was like she was truly seeing him in a new light. He felt her interest and her excitement.

For his little heart.

And the glow of her admiration dulled the fresh pain on his side as he dropped the hem of his shirt.

He shrugged, as he felt his face blush. "Yeah, well, thanks, Daisy."

★ ★ ★

Danny walked home after school in a daze as he stared at his cell phone in his hand. He actually had Daisy Zayland's number.

She'd taken his phone and added herself as a contact. Then he'd given his number to her.

Now they could text. They could talk.

About body art.

He'd get to know her better. They'd start to talk all the time. Maybe they'd eventually go out on a date. Maybe to the movies. They could share a popcorn. Maybe she'd truly start to like him.

Maybe one day . . .

She could become his first girlfriend.

Oh wow, everything would be so perfect.

"Hey, Danny, wait up!"

Danny turned to see Aaron running to catch up with him. Aaron's breaths were gushing through his mouth. He pulled out his inhaler for a puff when he reached him.

"Wh-What happened? Why didn't you wait for me after school?" His shoulders were moving up and down with exertion.

Danny's mouth gaped. He couldn't believe he forgot to wait for Aaron. "Oh, sorry, Aaron. I guess I forgot."

"Are you serious? We walk home every day together!" Aaron gave him a strange look. "What did you end up doing at lunch?"

"Oh, yeah." Danny smiled big. "I went to the library and I actually ran into Daisy Zayland. *We talked.*" He nodded his head and clarified, "To each other."

Aaron's eyes widened in surprise; his thick eyebrows inched up. "You finally talked to her? What'd she say?"

Danny decided to leave out the part about the little heart. "She gave me her number. Look!" He showed him her contact in his phone.

Aaron's eyebrows seemed to raise even more. "She gave *you* her number?"

Danny nodded, excited. "Amazing, right? *Me*. What do you think I should text her first? Or should I wait for her to text me? And if she does, should I text back right away? Or wait a little bit to show I'm not too anxious?"

Aaron shook his head in disbelief as they walked home. "I don't know. I'm still stuck on the fact that she gave *you* her number."

Danny only half-listened to Aaron on the short walk home. In his mind, he was reeling that Daisy Zayland had talked to him and had given him her number, and at the same time he was trying to figure out what went wrong with the bots, and how he got carved with the heart instead of the design drawn onto his skin.

He absently waved a good-bye to Aaron when they got to their street corner to part ways and then he started to run home, his backpack hitting his back. Something was weird and he needed to understand what had happened.

Danny unlocked the front door, slammed it shut, rushed to his room—he didn't see anyone home—and pulled out last night's pants from the laundry basket. He scanned the lining of the pockets he'd found empty the night before. This time he noticed two tiny, perfect holes in the lining of the pocket where he had put the bots.

The circles looked as if they'd been cut.

Cut . . .

His eyes widened as he pictured the wrapping paper being trimmed to the perfect size to wrap the presents at the Giftplex. How the ribbon was twirled and sliced into decorative bows.

Could there have been two types of mini bots in the gift wrapping booth? he wondered. One type for the drawing and coloring and another kind for the cutting?

He hurried to his desk, opened a junk drawer, and rummaged around for a tiny magnifying glass from his sixth-grade science camp. *Got it.* He grabbed the tiny glass and quickly unbuttoned his pants, shoved his pants down to his ankles, and stood in his spaceship underwear as he scanned his legs with the magnifying glass. *There.* On his right thigh were two tiny marks. Big enough for bots the size of a grain of rice to slip through.

He raised his head in disbelief and the magnifying glass slipped from his fingers.

The bots had cut into his body.

The bots were *inside* of him.

"Oh wow, oh wow, oh no."

His heart pounded hard in his chest and his face suddenly felt very hot. His hand went to his forehead.

His stomach pitched and flipped over. His other hand went to his stomach.

Out of all the bots, he took the wrong ones. He took the cutters instead of the painters.

And now they were inside of his body.

Able to cut into . . . *anything.*

"Uhhhhhh, wow, I think I'm going to throw up."

His body jerked as liquid gushed up his throat. He slapped a hand to his mouth and tripped over his pants around his ankles. He shoved to his feet and half ran, half slid, to the bathroom.

He made it to the toilet just in time to blow chunks.

That evening, Danny told his mom he didn't feel good and stayed in bed through dinner. There was no way he could even think of eating at a time like this. His stomach was raw and upset. His hip was sore and itchy where the little heart was cut into him. He felt exhausted. He'd done something incredibly dumb—by accident—but he'd still done it.

And he didn't know how he was going to fix it. His mind was whirling with uncertainty and fear. What was he going to do? How did you get tiny robots out of your body?

He even tried the question on an internet search.

Body scan. X-ray. Surgery.

He doubted the little cutter bots were even big enough to be detected.

He ran a frustrated hand over his face. Oh wow, he messed up so bad.

He wished his dad was home. Maybe he could call him and at least talk a little with him. Talking to his dad always made him feel good when he was down. He wouldn't be able to tell him exactly what happened. Who would really believe him? But his dad had a way of ensuring him that everything was going to work out in the long run.

He grabbed his cell phone from his side table and dialed his dad's number. After a few rings, the voice mail recording came on.

He closed his eyes and took a breath. "Hi, Dad. Um, it's Danny. I just wanted to talk to you. But, I guess you're working . . . Could you call me back? I can't wait till you come home. I miss you. Okay. Love you. Bye."

Danny clicked off the call, set the phone aside, and curled up in his bed. His stomach was twirling like a washing machine.

Eventually, he fell asleep.

"Honey, wake up."

Danny blinked awake to see his mom leaning over his bed. Her brown eyes looked worried. He could smell her rose perfume. "Are you feeling okay, hun? Dad said you left a message on his voice mail. Is everything okay?"

He rubbed his eyes. Did he miss Dad's call? He reached for his cell phone on his side table. There was no missed call or a message from his dad.

"Why didn't he call me?" Danny asked groggily.

"You know he's busy with work, hun. He checked in with me this morning and mentioned your call." She felt his head with her hand. "You don't have a fever. Is it your stomach again?"

He shook his head. His stomach seemed to be all right at the moment. "No, I'm okay. I'm getting up to go to school."

"'Kay, just take it easy. Tarts will be on the table for you."

He nodded his head and his mom walked out of his bedroom. "Bobby, you up?" she called out.

"Yeah, Ma," Bobby answered from down the hallway.

So his dad didn't get a chance to call him back, Danny realized. Like Mom said, he was busy with work. As usual. Danny buried the heavy disappointment he felt in his chest and sat up on his bed. He would be okay with the tiny bots inside of his body for now, he told himself.

He hoped.

That morning, he walked to school with Aaron, listening to him talk about the latest graphic novels that he still hadn't picked up. He shrugged when Aaron asked him if he could talk about them. So Aaron had jumped at the chance to share the entire plots on the way to school.

"Can you believe it? Cool ending, huh? I can't wait for the next issues." When Danny didn't respond, he asked him, "Hey, Danny, is everything okay?"

Danny nodded as he stepped inside the entrance of the school and made his way to his locker. "Fine. I just . . ."

"What?"

He shrugged uncomfortably. "Kinda miss my dad."

Aaron looked down and nodded. "Oh, I get it. My dad sometimes goes on business trips and we miss him when he's gone. And it's so close to Christmas. But on the upside, you'll see him soon, yeah?" Aaron gave him an encouraging smile.

Danny forced his lips to curve. "Yeah, you're right." He just wished his dad called him back.

"Okay, well, I'll see you at lunch."

"Okay, see you." Danny exchanged his books in his locker, closed the door, and turned.

Daisy stood in front of him, hugging her binder in front of her. "Hi," she said with a smile.

Danny straightened his shoulders, his pulse spiking as a smile curved his lips. "Oh hi, Daisy."

"I got some new body art magazines in the mail. Want to look at them at lunch with me?"

Fresh excitement rushed through Danny, making him feel a little better about his dad not calling him back. "Sure, yeah, that sounds good."

She lifted her eyebrows. "So I'll see you in the library?"

He nodded. "Yep. I'll be there."

"Okay, see you then." She turned around just as the first morning bell rang.

Daisy Zayland actually wanted to hang out with him at school! This was amazing. He thought of Aaron. Oh, he would understand, he reasoned, as he took out his cell phone to text him that he was busy at lunch and that he'd see him after school.

"So which tattoos do you like?" Daisy asked him from across the table in the library. She had two magazines. She was looking through one and Danny was skimming through the other.

"They are all pretty cool," he said.

"I know, but what would you get if you could get one?" She took out her cell phone and took a couple photos of tattoos she liked. One was of a humming bird and the other was a little kitten.

The truth was, Danny could get any of these tattoos, but they would be etched instead of inked. *Wonder what Daisy would think about that? She is a girl,* he reasoned, *so she might gross out.*

Right then the little heart on his hip started to itch again and he scratched at it.

"The animal ones, but I might try and draw one of my own designs and see what I can come up with."

Daisy flipped her hair back with her hand. "You draw?"

He blinked and realized Daisy knew nothing about him. She didn't even know it had been him who drew the pictures of her that she found in her locker.

Considering she crumbled up the latest one and threw it away, he wasn't about to tell her it had been him, either.

He nodded. "Yeah, I like to draw."

"I should have known with that drawing pencil on your ear." She smiled at him and Danny felt a warm glow in his chest.

He smiled back. "Good observation skills."

"Could you draw the tattoo you would get if you could?"

Danny nodded. "Sure, I could."

The bell rang for lunch to be over. "Great! Draw a tattoo design and show me tomorrow."

"Okay, I will."

After school, Danny walked home with Aaron, listening to him talk about his music class.

"Then Hank Mason hit Charlie Cooper in the nose with his clarinet. By accident, but the entire class started busting up laughing. Mrs. Jimenez was not amused, though. Oh, and Katie Howard freaked out when a spider crawled out of her violin case . . ."

Danny didn't say much as Aaron talked. He kept replaying his lunch with Daisy in his mind. She really was so pretty. And she was nice, too. How could Aaron even think she was snobby?

As soon as they got to their corner to part ways, Danny waved good-bye and rushed off to his house.

"See you tomorrow, Danny!" Aaron called out.

When Danny got home, he went straight to his room

and pulled his sketchbook out from his backpack. He plopped onto his bed and started to draw a grizzly bear. He had always admired bears since he had to do a report on them in fifth grade. They were big and strong and independent. Something that Danny wished he would be someday. Minus the having to hunt for his food and shelter.

He sketched a big grizzly bear in a graphic-novel style with thick lines and no shading. It didn't take him as long as he thought. When he was done, he gazed at his drawing. It was pretty good, he realized. Probably one of his best.

Maybe spending time with Daisy really inspired my artwork, he thought. It sure felt like it!

"I do want a tattoo like this, probably right on my shoulder." As soon as he said it, his stomach pitched. "*Wait.* I mean, one day! Not now!"

Too late.

A sharp cut pierced his skin on his right shoulder. He yelped as the bots sliced into him. He grabbed at his arm and fell to the floor. Sweat pearled on his forehead as he felt the wetness of blood pool under his shirt while the mini knives carved and scraped.

"Please, no, I didn't mean it! Stop!"

But the cutting didn't cease and seemed to go on and on. A tear ran down his cheek and then another.

The pain was *so bad.*

He thought he was going to pass out from the agony . . .

Until, *finally,* the bots unexpectedly stopped and the cutting pain turned into a steady throbbing.

Breathing hard, he rolled onto his back on the carpet as he felt blood drip down his arm. *He messed up again.*

He ran a hand down his face and wiped away his sweat and tears.

He laid there another moment, and then slowly got up and pulled off his hoodie. Streaks of blood ran down his arm as he hesitantly lifted the sleeve of his T-shirt. There on his shoulder was the bear design carved into his skin that he'd just sketched.

He lifted his eyebrows because if it had been a real tattoo it would have looked really good, but as a bloody injury it was a painful mess.

"I have to be more careful with what I say." Then he got up and walked to the bathroom to clean up before anyone came home. When he walked out of the bathroom, sore, tired, and patched up with some gauze, he glanced down at his bloody shirt.

The blood! If his mom found all the blood stains on his clothes, she would freak out!

He quickly grabbed the shirt he was wearing when he got the first little heart and the hoodie he wore earlier, then took off his shirt that had blood on it, and he rushed to the laundry room. He rinsed out the bloody spots as best as he could in the sink and then placed everything in the wash with some laundry soap.

He sighed in relief when he started the wash cycle.

Everything is going to be okay, he told himself.

Then he heard the key rattle in the front door. He ran to his room to shut the door before anyone noticed his patched-up shoulder.

The next day at school, Daisy walked up to his locker while Aaron was still with him.

"Hi, Danny," she said.

"Hi, Daisy, um, this is Aaron," Danny said. "You already know him."

Aaron said, "Hi."

Daisy tilted her head, gave Aaron a brief glance, and looked away. "No, I don't know him."

"We have fourth period together," Aaron told her.

"Oh, really?" Daisy shrugged. "So, Danny, did you make the drawing we talked about?"

Danny nodded. He pulled out his sketchbook from his backpack and turned to the page with the bear illustration.

"Oh, that's really cool!" Daisy gushed.

Danny smiled. "Yeah, you like it?"

She nodded. "I could definitely see that as a tattoo."

"A tattoo?" Aaron interrupted, with a scrunched-up face. "I think you have a while till that happens. Anyway, why would you want to mess up your body like that?"

Daisy rolled her eyes. "Tattooing is a form of artistic self-expression, Eric."

Aaron's thick eyebrows pushed toward each other. "I told you, it's Aaron. Tattooing is also very painful and expensive. I've seen stuff online."

"And that's supposed to make you such an expert or something?" Daisy snapped back. "It's only painful for those who can't handle the pain." She smiled at Danny. "But Danny can handle it, right, Danny? And of course, I can since I have an actual tattoo."

Aaron laughed. "Danny used to cry when he scraped his knee. There's no way he could handle the pain of getting a real tattoo."

"That's what you think, Alec." Daisy smiled at Danny, as if hinting at their little secret.

"Aaron," Aaron grumbled.

Danny gave Aaron a look. "All right, Aaron, don't you have to get to your locker before class?"

Aaron flinched in surprise. "Oh, I guess." He glanced uncertainly at Daisy and then Danny. "I'll see you at lunch."

"You're not coming to the library today, Danny?" Daisy asked.

Danny cleared his throat. "Um, well . . . ."

"Library? Is that where you went yesterday?" Aaron asked him.

"Yes, we hang out together at lunch now," Daisy boldly told Aaron. "Just the two of us, and we talk all about tattoos. Something you're obviously not very interested in, Alvin."

"Aaron," Aaron corrected again absently, pointing a thumb at Daisy. "Is that true, Danny? You want to hang out with her at lunch and talk about tattoos?"

Danny shifted uncomfortably on his feet. "I guess. I mean, I want to hang out with both—"

"Fine." Aaron pulled out his inhaler and took a puff. "Do whatever you want. I got something to do, anyway." Then he turned around and stalked away.

"Hey, Aaron!" Danny called out as guilt weighed on him. "Hold on!"

But his best friend didn't stop to look back and soon disappeared into the hallway crowd.

"Just let him go, Danny," Daisy said. "You can see him later."

Danny felt bad. But he would see Aaron after school and try to explain how good it was to have Daisy want to talk and spend time with him. In fact, it felt really great. Aaron probably didn't get it because he didn't have a crush like Danny had on Daisy.

"Come on, you can walk me to class." She placed a hand on his shoulder.

Danny recoiled at her touch. "Ow!"

Daisy snatched back her hand. "What? What happened? I barely touched you."

Danny grabbed tentatively at as his shoulder. "Um, it's nothing."

Then she slowly smiled. "You did it again, didn't you?"

Danny sighed. "Well, kinda."

Her eyes widened in excitement and Danny's heart swelled with her gleeful attention. "Come on, show me."

The first bell rang. "Maybe at lunch?"

She nodded. "Meet me at the track field at lunch. I can't wait to see it!"

Danny gave a hesitant smile. "I think you'll really like it."

"Oh my gosh, Danny, did it hurt?" Daisy stared in awe at the rawness of the shoulder as he showed her far off in the corner of the school's track field. Kids roamed the field but far enough away from them that they couldn't see the bear cut in Danny's skin.

Did it hurt? The painful incident flashed back through his mind. "Yeah, a little."

"This is so awesome! How are you doing this? The lines are just so perfect and precise."

"Um, well, it's something like a trade secret."

She looked at him. "A secret? Come on, you have to tell me! Friends don't have secrets from each other."

"Friends?" Danny asked with a smile. He was now real friends with Daisy Zayland. This was so fantastic.

She eagerly stepped closer and Danny could smell her floral shampoo. "Yeah, so tell me."

He closed his eyes a moment because she smelled so good, but he just shook his head and placed the gauze back on his shoulder with the tape. There was no way she would believe him. "Maybe later."

She frowned but waved a hand in the air. "Fine, are you going to do more of these?"

Danny swallowed hard. "Uh, I think I'll take a little break. It takes a lot of . . . hard work."

She nodded. "If it was me, you wouldn't be able to stop me from getting more. It's such a drag I have to wait for my parents to get back from their business trips or when they aren't too busy to take me."

"Your parents travel a lot?"

She nodded. "Yeah, I have to stay with a nanny."

"You have a nanny?"

Her cheeks flushed pink. "Well, she was my nanny since I was little. And she still stays with me when my parents travel. Her name is Ms. Gladys. I mean, I tell my parents I'm old enough to stay home on my own, but they feel bet-ter with her staying with me. Anyways, that was why they finally caved and let me get a tattoo. They wanted it to be okay with me that they travel all the time. They promised to let me get another one."

"You don't have any siblings, either?"

She shook her head.

Danny nodded. "Well, that's understandable. It's not safe to stay alone. My dad has to travel all the time for his job. But I'll be able to see him soon at Christmas. You'll see your parents soon, too."

She shrugged. "They're actually stopping somewhere to go skiing."

Danny blinked in surprise. "You mean, you won't be going with them?"

She looked out at the track field, her cheeks blushing. "Well, they're already traveling, so it was easier for them to stop at a resort, and then they'll see me after Christmas."

Danny couldn't believe she wouldn't be with her parents on Christmas. At least Danny had his mom home all the time with him and his brothers. He suddenly felt really bad for Daisy.

Aaron was so wrong about her. She wasn't snobby. She just didn't have a lot of friends and she hardly even had her parents home with her. Danny understood how much he missed his dad when he was away. To have both parents gone so often had to be really rough.

Maybe Danny was Daisy's only friend. He didn't really see her talking to other kids around school.

Daisy looked at him a little shyly for the first time. "I mean, at least I have my interest in tattoos to keep me busy. And now, I have you to talk with, right?"

"Yeah, of course. You can count on me. Anytime. When you need me, I'll be there." A feeling of pride bloomed in his chest. In a way, Daisy needed him, and he decided then and there that he would take the responsibility of being her only friend very seriously.

She smiled. "Great! Let's think of something you can get next."

Danny hesitated, but only for a second. He told her he

wanted to take a break but considering his type of body art made her happy, he was willing to get a little more to help her keep her mind off her parents not coming home for Christmas.

As her only friend, he had to try and make her happy.

"Okay," he told her as they started across the track field, "help me think of ideas for my next one."

Danny's next skin design was of a hummingbird because Daisy liked them so much. He prepared this time by stashing old towels and garbage bags under his bed in his room for easier cleanup. Unfortunately, the pain wasn't getting any easier to endure. In fact, it felt even worse with each cutting the bots performed. His heart felt like it wanted to pound right out of his chest. His body would tremble and sweat as the blood dripped out of his body. And when the cutting stopped, he was super exhausted. He hadn't been able to get up to patch himself for at least fifteen minutes.

But he was able to get through it knowing Daisy would love the design so much.

Being with Daisy made him feel noticed and wanted. Something he hadn't felt in a while, not since Johnny was born. He knew his parents loved him, but being with Daisy felt different. She made him feel needed in some weird way, and she made his nerves tingle whenever he was with her. He'd never felt like that before, and he wanted to hold on to the feeling as long as he could.

The next day, he took her again to the far corner of the track field so no one could see or hear what they were talking about. He started to feel like Blake Billings in the graphic novels he liked to read, with an alternate persona.

This time, he had the hummingbird etched onto his other shoulder.

Daisy gasped. "Danny, I love it! You're the coolest! No one has ever done something so unique for me before!" Daisy clasped her fingers together and actually hopped up in excitement.

Daisy's admiration and joy zipped through Danny like a spurt of sugar. "I'm so glad you like it."

"Oh my gosh, you are like the coolest friend I've ever had!"

Danny envisioned himself jumping for joy and performing a bunch of cartwheels in his head. For a girl like Daisy to praise him was like catching a rainbow!

"Do you think you can do one on me?" she asked out of the blue.

Danny's thrill faded away as he slowly placed the gauze back on his shoulder and dropped the sleeve of his shirt. "Oh no. Um, it's really hard to do and pretty painful."

"I can take it. I'll get a small one like the star on my wrist. Come on, it'll be really cool."

"No!" Danny said a little too sternly. "I can't, Daisy."

"Why not?"

He shook his head adamantly. "I just can't."

"Oh, fine." Daisy looked away at the track field, and crossed her arms. "Be that way." There was a moment of silence as she glanced at her nails. "Well, I have to go. I forgot I had something to do. I forgot I told someone I would meet with them."

Danny's stomach pitched as panic set in. "Wait, Daisy." He reached out awkwardly for her but didn't touch her. "You're meeting someone else?" When she just shrugged, he went on, "I mean, it's hard enough to do this to myself. I'm not ready to, um, work on others. I'm not there yet if you know what I mean. What I go through . . . it's not easy at all. It's pretty complex."

Daisy turned back to him, her eyes downcast. "Yeah, I guess I get it."

"You just have to wait a little while," he fibbed. He didn't really know what else to say but he didn't want her to walk away upset with him. He finally had Daisy Zayland's attention. He would do anything to keep her as his friend. If Daisy didn't want to be his friend anymore, it would crush him into tiny bits.

She finally nodded and met his gaze. "But when you are ready, let me know. I want to be the first one to get your work. Okay?"

Danny relaxed a little. "Sure. Definitely. When I'm ready." Which in reality, he'd never be. But at least she still wanted to hang out with him.

She gave a small smile. "Okay, let's talk about your next one."

"Yeah, um, so who else were you going to meet?"

"Oh, just some kid. No one important."

Later after school on the walk home, Aaron would barely look at Danny let alone talk to him. And Aaron always wanted to talk. Danny knew he was still upset about Danny ditching him at lunch to spend time with Daisy.

There was a chilled breeze blowing in dark clouds, and Danny wondered if it was going to rain soon. But he doubted Aaron wanted to talk about the weather.

He pulled the pencil from his ear and started to tap

his palm with it. "Aaron, I know you're upset about me spending my lunches with Daisy."

"I told you to do whatever you want," Aaron muttered.

"I know, it's just I want you to understand. I like her and it feels good that she wants to hang out with me. I want you to understand."

"I get it. You have a girlfriend now."

Danny's eyes widened as he slipped the pencil back on top of his ear, and he smiled at the potential idea of being Daisy's boyfriend. "What? No, no! Daisy's not my girlfriend." *Hopefully, one day.* "I mean, we're just friends. We talk about tattoos and stuff."

Aaron shook his head. "That's what I don't get. Why are you so into tattoos all of a sudden? I mean, you like art, but you like graphic novels and illustrations. Then Daisy Zayland comes along and you change what you like."

"I haven't changed. I'm still me. I just—"

"Like tattoos now." Aaron shook his head. "She's just using you."

Danny frowned. "What do you mean? Using me for what?"

"She doesn't have any friends because she's so stuck up and everyone around school thinks so. Except you. She's using you so she's not such a loner, and once someone better or cooler comes along, she'll dump you."

"That's not true, Aaron. Daisy isn't like that. And just because I hang out with her, doesn't mean you're not my best friend anymore."

Aaron didn't say anything as they stopped at the corner where they split up.

"So I'll see you tomorrow?" Danny asked him hesitantly.

Aaron was staring down at the ground. "Maybe." Then he turned and took off for home.

Danny felt bad again, watching Aaron walk away, swinging his flute case. *It isn't true what he said about Daisy*, Danny told himself. *It's not using someone when the person wants to hang out with you, too, right?*

Then his phone pinged with a text. It was Daisy.

She wanted him to draw a tattoo of a black cat.

Danny smiled as he headed home. *Anything for you, Daisy.*

Danny drew the cat design in his sketchbook. This time he shaded the drawing in with all black. *Daisy will love this one*, he thought, satisfied. It was like with each body modification, Daisy was drawn more and more to him and he to her, connecting them in a way he never thought possible. It was like he couldn't get enough time with her. He could feel himself wanting to please her more each day . . .

There was a knock on his bedroom door. He wasn't sure why but he slammed his sketchbook shut and called out, "Yeah?"

The door opened, and his mom came in with some folded laundry. "Danny, you did some of your own wash?" She had a pleased smiled on her face. "What brought this on?"

"Oh," he said, as his face heated. "Uh, yeah, I got some . . . um . . . paint on them and didn't want them to stain." He looked down at his carpeted floor. It was speckled with various colors, and he suddenly spotted a drop of blood.

Oh no! He looked quickly at his mom, but she wasn't looking at the floor.

"Good call, hun. Thanks for saving me the work. Next time, you can put a few more pieces in the load so it's not so small. 'Kay?"

"Sure." He nodded as his gut tightened with the fibs he was telling his mom. He hadn't really lied to her since he was little and hadn't wanted to get in trouble for coloring on the walls with crayons.

She patted his shoulder and he did his best not to cringe. Both of his shoulders were healing and still so sore.

"You're a good boy, Danny," she said, with a smile. "Never give me any trouble. Since you're being so helpful, I could use some help in the kitchen with dinner."

"Sure, Mom." He released a breath when she let go of him. "I'll be right there."

Once his mom walked out of his room, he fell to the ground and tried to wipe the drip of blood with his hand. The stain was dried so he decided to spit on it, then he rubbed at the spot with his open palm. It smeared a little and didn't look like blood anymore.

That will have to do, he thought.

Danny sprang to his feet and rushed out of his room to help his mom. He washed his hands and helped with the dinner salad, while she boiled pasta and cooked the sauce for the spaghetti. A short while later, they all sat down for their family dinner with his brothers.

Danny listened to Bobby take over the conversation about school and how his teachers loved him. Just like always.

"Of course, they love you, hun," Mom told Bobby. "You're such a good and helpful student."

Bobby smiled and Danny rolled his eyes.

His brother caught him and narrowed his eyes at Danny.

Mom's cell phone rang. "Oh, it's Daddy." She answered the call and clicked on the speaker. "Hi, hun, we're all here finishing up dinner."

"Hey kids!" Dad greeted them.

"Hi Dad!" Bobby said.

"'Addy! 'Addy!" Johnny shouted.

"Hi, Dad," Danny greeted him.

"What's new with everyone?" Dad asked.

"Danny has a crush on a girl at school!" Bobby shouted, his shoulders shaking with a quiet laugh.

Danny's eyes widened in shock. His face went hot. "Shut up, Bobby!"

"You like someone, Danny?" his mom asked. "That's so sweet."

"No!" Danny yelled, ready to fling spaghetti at his brother, but he was pretty sure he'd get busted for that.

"Yes, he does!" Bobby went on. "He was asking me for advice! Wanted to know how to get her to notice him. So being a good big brother, I told him."

"Oh really, you're an expert, are you, Bobby?" Mom asked with a smile in her voice.

"You remember I had that girlfriend in ninth grade. Nancy Dawson."

"Hmmm. Lasted a week, as I recall," Dad said, also with a slight lilt in his voice.

"Anyway," Bobby said. "I felt I was qualified enough to help out my little brother."

All Danny could do was deny it even happened although that was completely true. He had wanted to talk to his dad about Daisy one-on-one. He had wanted to be the one to tell him. Not his selfish older brother who had to take the spotlight all the time, even when it didn't have anything to do with him. He should have never told him anything!

"Aw, our middle boy is growing up, Pat," his mom said, giving Danny a funny look.

"Bobby has a big mouth and he needs to shut up!" Danny yelled.

"Danny, come on now," his mom scolded. "Be nice."

"It's okay, Danny," his dad said through the phone. "It's natural to have crushes. You're growing up, son. I bet she's a nice girl."

"Her name's Daisy," Bobby spat out.

Danny's back teeth ground together. "Well, can anyone tell me when Bobby is finally going to grow up?!" Angry, he shoved back from the table, grabbed his plate, and stormed into the kitchen. His face was so hot and his chest felt tight. He scraped off his plate with the fork, set them in the sink, and stormed to his room.

He closed the door and locked it, then yanked open his sketchbook. He stared at the cat drawing, and his nostrils flared. "I want this cat on my stomach."

The bots got to work immediately.

Danny keeled over and fell to the floor onto his knees as the tiny knives dug into his skin. "Ahhhhhh," he moaned. His body began to tremble and shake as the pain increased and increased. Blood poured out of his stomach and he rolled onto his back as he curled up with the pain.

What's happening?

The cutting was even worse. He wanted to scream, but he covered his mouth as tears ran down his face.

Make it stop! Make it stop!

A couple of torturous minutes later, the bots finally finished. Danny's shoulders were heaving and his nose was running. He wiped at his face and snot stuck to his hand. *Ugh.*

He sat up carefully and it seemed like more blood pooled out of his gut onto his jeans.

Oh wow, oh wow.

Something was seriously wrong.

He carefully lifted his shirt and a red blob of something fell onto his lap.

Danny flinched in surprise. "*Gross.* What is that?"

He carefully picked up the blob with his fingers as his eyes widened. It was the cat he'd drawn!

The bots had cut out an entire piece of flesh from his stomach! The flesh was thin and flabby. He started to shake as he raised his other hand to his bleeding stomach.

"Oh no. Too far," he murmured as he grew lightheaded. "I've gone too far." He grabbed some of the old hand towels and a garbage bag from under his bed and started to clean himself up. He threw all the bloody red towels in the bag and looked at the flesh carving of his stomach. It looked as if someone had used a cookie cutter the shape of a cat on his skin. Luckily, it hadn't been too deep or he didn't know what he would do.

He threw the piece of flesh in the bag and then slipped out of his bloody clothes and threw them into the garbage bag as well. There was no way he could get all the blood out of them without someone noticing.

He felt really off. Weak. When he stood to put on

some fresh clothes, black dots flashed in front of his eyes. He balanced out his arms so he wouldn't fall over and faint.

He probably lost too much blood.

"I'm okay," he whispered. "I can handle this. I just went a little too far this time. Lesson learned."

Now he knew when he blacked out the entire design, the bots cut the whole thing out of his body. "Good to know." He slowly dressed in some sweats and stuffed the garbage bag deep into the closet to throw away tomorrow. Then he heard his mom call out to get ready for bed.

Dizzy, Danny fell to his bed, holding his spinning head.

He just needed a minute to rest before he bandaged himself.

He couldn't get up for the next hour.

The next morning, Danny forced himself to walk to school as cold air puffed from his mouth. It had ended up raining the night before and the sidewalks and streets were dotted with puddles. He felt really under the weather. Weak and tired. He hadn't felt like getting up in the morning, but when his mom called for everyone to get out of bed, he got up, anyway. His stomach was empty because the sight of the breakfast tarts made him gag so he hadn't eaten them. He'd just tossed them in the garbage and covered them up so his mom wouldn't know.

When Danny reached the corner to meet Aaron, his best friend wasn't there. Danny was surprised and a little hurt. Was he ditching him because he was mad?

Maybe he'd hurt Aaron's feelings.

Danny wasn't sure how he'd feel if it had been Aaron who wanted to hang out with someone else. But he would have at least tried to grasp how Aaron felt. Aaron wasn't even trying.

Why couldn't Aaron understand how Daisy made him feel? How she gave him so much of her attention and admiration. Something he rarely got from anyone else. Yeah, Danny didn't know if it was *only* for his special body art from the bots. But still, he didn't care.

All he cared about was being with Daisy and making her happy so *he* could feel good.

Danny figured he would make amends with his best friend eventually. Maybe he could buy him something as a peace offering, like his favorite candy bar or something.

They were best friends, after all. He had to forgive him, right?

Danny walked the rest of the way to school, shivering from the cold. It was as if he couldn't get warm even though he wore an extra rain jacket over his sweatshirt. When he reached the school grounds, he pulled out the garbage bag from his backpack and threw it into the dumpster in the parking lot. His breaths were fast and he felt exhausted just from throwing the bag into the bin. He walked into school to find Daisy waiting for him at his locker. There was still no sign of Aaron.

"Danny, look!" she told him, excited. "It's a Body Art Expo in town! Can you believe it? We have to go!"

Danny glanced at the flyer Daisy waved in front of his face.

"Wow, looks really cool," he told her, but she was making him dizzy waving the flyer around.

"It's tomorrow. Will your mom let you go?"

"Well, um, it's a Saturday. She shouldn't say no since we're also starting our holiday break." Although, he wasn't sure his mom would let him go to a tattoo expo with a bunch of strange adults. He might have to think of another plan in order to get out of the house for a couple of hours.

"Danny," she said suddenly, studying his face, "you're so pale."

Danny nodded, a little embarrassed. "Yeah, it's from—"

"I know and it's so cool, Danny. It just shows how dedicated you are to body art. I really admire that about you."

"You do?" Danny blinked. "You think I'm dedicated?"

She smiled at him and touched his hand. "I know so."

Danny actually felt a flutter in his chest. He swallowed hard. "Thanks, Daisy. You're the best."

Daisy tossed her hair with a smile. "Thanks! So did you draw the cat tatt?"

He nodded, mesmerized by the fact that Daisy had actually touched his hand.

"Can't wait till you get that one on you."

He laughed nervously. "Uh, yeah. Can't wait. Anything for you, Daisy."

"Hey, Mom, is it okay if I go to Aaron's today? Um, he wants to hang out. We haven't been able to for a while." Danny shifted on his feet. His pulse was fluttering from lying. It was Saturday morning and Danny and his brothers were officially on holiday break from school.

Mom was busy washing the breakfast dishes. She was in sweats and a sweatshirt, and her brown hair was pulled back in a bun.

She glanced at Danny. "Are his parents going to be home?"

Danny nodded. "Yeah, of course."

"Then it should be okay." She squinted her eyes at him. "Danny, you're awfully pale. Are you still not feeling well? Do we need to make you an appointment for a checkup?"

"No, no. You know the sun hasn't been out in days." Which was true. The weather had been cold and overcast for a couple of weeks.

"Okay, but try not to stay too long. You look like you could use some rest, hun."

"Sure, Mom."

Yeah, Danny needed rest. He'd stood in his pajama shorts in front of the bathroom mirror that morning in complete shock. He hardly recognized himself. His body was carved up in four places with different designs that were still healing with red and itchy scabs. There was even bruising around some of the recent designs. His face was super pale and he had dark circles under his eyes. His cheeks and gut looked sunken in. He wasn't sure how much more he could keep cutting into his skin without getting really sick.

When he met Daisy at the Body Art Expo, he'd have to tell her he couldn't do it anymore. Or that he had to at least take a break.

But there was a little voice inside him that told him his greatest fear . . .

Then she won't be your friend anymore.

Mom's cell phone rang. She turned off the faucet and dried her hands with a dish towel. "Oh, it's Dad." She answered her cell phone. "Hey, hun. How you doing? What?!" Her eyes brightened. "That's wonderful! When's the flight?" She glanced at the clock on the wall. "Oh, that's soon. The boys will be thrilled! I gotta go and get us ready." She laughed. "Yes, yes, see you soon, hun!" She clicked off the phone with a big smile. "Boys! Good news. Dad's coming home early!"

Bobby and Johnny rushed into the kitchen. "What's going on?" Bobby asked.

"Dad surprised us with an earlier flight. He's coming home *today*! We have to all drive to the airport to get him. Let's get ready to go! Hurry, hurry!"

"All right!" Bobby shouted, while Johnny started screaming in excitement as he ran to get ready.

While Danny was happy, he was also torn. He'd told Daisy he'd go to the expo with her, but he wanted to see his dad, too!

If he disappointed Daisy, she'd be so mad at him. She might not even speak to him again. Panic clawed in his gut at the idea. No, he couldn't disappoint her. He didn't even want to think about not having Daisy in his life. He was her only friend, after all. In a way, it was as if she only had Danny to depend on. Even though he wanted to go with his family, he'd be able to see his dad when they both got home. Daisy only had her nanny to go home to.

Danny followed his mom to her bedroom before she

closed the door. "Um, Mom, I'm not going to go with you guys to pick up dad."

Her eyes widened. "What? You haven't seen your father in three weeks."

"I know." He swallowed hard. "It's just I promised D—Aaron and I don't want him to get upset with me."

"Oh, I think he would understand. Aaron's a good friend."

"Maybe, but I'll see dad when he gets home. Is that okay?"

She cupped his chin. "You sure, hun?"

For some reason, his throat thickened. "Yeah. I'll see him soon. It'll only be a couple of hours."

"Okay." She smiled. "I'm so excited he's coming home early."

Danny smiled. "Me too."

Danny rushed over to meet Daisy at the entrance of the tattoo expo. He was running late because he had to wait till his mom and brothers left the house since he had to walk in the opposite direction from Aaron's house and take a bus to the Body Art Expo at the town conference center. He hoped Daisy wasn't mad at him for being late, but his brothers were driving him crazy as usual, singing a song that he was a party pooper for not coming with them. Bobby was so immature and Johnny kept singing along with him!

"There you are!" Daisy shouted at him after he ran through the parking lot to get to the main entrance of the building. "I was beginning to think you were standing me up!"

Danny had to catch his breath. "No, no, never." He

swallowed and realized his mouth was dry. "Sorry! Something came up at home, but I'm here now. Let's go in."

Daisy's annoyance fell away when she pulled out the neon-yellow wristbands. "Okay, here's yours. This is going to be so cool, Danny! I'm really excited. I kept thinking about it all night."

So did I, Danny thought. All he could think about was being with her.

Danny slipped on his wristband and took a breath. "Yeah, can't wait to see all the different styles of artists."

"Me too." Daisy offered her hand and Danny's eyes widened. He smiled at her, wiped his damp hand on his sweatshirt, and took her hand in his. It felt petite and warm.

Daisy was actually holding his hand. Daisy really liked him as much as he liked her!

He couldn't wait to draw their hands together just like this. He walked in holding the girl of his dream's hand. He was the luckiest kid in the world.

Daisy scanned everywhere inside the large conference center. She'd never been to the Body Art Expo before and there was so much excitement! So much creative energy. An actual punk rock band played loud music on a stage. People of all ages walked around, some with tattoos on their arms and necks and some even on their faces and shaved heads! She was mesmerized. Impressed. One day, she might have her entire body tattooed. She wondered what her parents would think about that!

They probably wouldn't even care, though. They were

always busy with their jobs and doing fun, grown-up things. It was like they didn't have time for Daisy at all.

Who cared, anyway. Look where she was? She was doing what made her happy for a change.

People were getting tattooed in booths. The buzzing of the tattoo guns filled the air. Others were getting facial piercings. A bunch of booths sold T-shirts, sweatshirts, and beanies. Another sold lotions to take care of your body art. There were people selling tattoo-styled paintings and various food and drink booths. And there were so many different styles of artists. She couldn't tell which artist she liked best.

This was *almost* the greatest day of her life! It would have been even more wonderful if she was actually eighteen and could get a tattoo instead of depending on her parents' permission!

One day.

"Have you seen anything as cool as this before?" she asked Danny.

Danny shook his head. "No, it's pretty amazing."

"Let's look over here!" She pulled Danny toward an artist selling tattoos and artwork. The artist had two eyebrow piercings, with both arms covered with full tattoo sleeves, and he was kind of cute for an old guy.

"Hey, there, you kids looking to get a tatt?" the tattoo artist asked.

"Well, I have one already." She let go of Danny's hand to show the artist the star tattoo on her wrist. "But I can't get another without my parents."

The artist nodded his head in understanding. "Ah, not eighteen yet."

She rolled her eyes. "It's such a silly law. I mean, I make my own decisions anyway, you know?"

"Well, if you can't get a tattoo, check out some of my artwork for sale. I have a lot of stickers and prints."

Daisy gazed around, excited she had a real tattoo artist's attention. "You are super talented. If I could, I would so get one of your tattoos right on my arm."

The tattoo artist smiled. "Thanks. Which design do you like the best?"

Danny cleared his throat, but Daisy ignored him. Couldn't he see she was having a serious, mature conversation here?

When he cleared his throat again, she turned to him. "Danny, I'm really thirsty. Could you get me a soda?" She knew Danny was always trying to please her. At first that's why she hung around him, and for the cool and different body art he was able to do on himself, but she found out he was a nice friend to talk with, too.

"Oh, sure," he told her. "Why don't you come with me so you can pick it out?"

"No, it's okay. I like grape."

Danny's shoulders sagged. "Okay. Well, I'll be right back."

She waved him off. "Take your time. There's no rush." She batted her eyelashes at the tattoo artist. "So which tattoo do you think would look good on me?"

Danny attempted to hurry back to Daisy. It had actually taken longer than he thought to get the grape soda. First, he couldn't find a booth that carried grape. Then, when he finally did, there had been a long line. He hoped he could find her quickly in the crowd.

However, it didn't take long to find Daisy because she was still at the *same* tattoo booth with that *same* creepy tattoo guy!

Danny's steps slowed.

Why did she want to talk with him so much?

She'd come to the expo with Danny, not the tattoo guy.

It was actually their first official outing together and she was giving all her attention to someone else.

That familiar feeling of being a nobody, someone unnoticed, came back in full force like a ton of bricks.

He'd thought Daisy was different. He'd thought they'd had a good relationship. One that was growing every day. He understood her. He kept doing the skin designs because that was what she wanted. He knew how she felt being ignored by her parents. He was the one who hung out with her, who became her only friend.

But maybe she only really cared about the skin designs all along.

Had Aaron been right about her?

Had Daisy just been using him until someone better came along?

No, this couldn't be happening. His heart felt like it was literally breaking. He should just go home. He should just leave her with the creepy tattoo artist.

The old guy could be her only friend.

Danny continued to walk straight to Daisy. He handed her the soda, ready to leave and walk away. His hand trembled. "Here."

"Oh thanks," she said, barely looking at him as she took the soda can.

The tattoo artist was showing her his book. "It's taken me years to hone my style and to build a portfolio I'm proud of."

"How did you choose all these tattoos on your arms?"

"I wanted each tatt to mean something. I didn't want to be one of those kids who gets tatts just to have them, you know?"

Daisy nodded eagerly, her eyelashes fluttering. "That's so cool. That's how I feel, too."

And something snapped in Danny.

All the attention she'd given to Danny was now given to this random guy.

Danny had lost her in a blink of an eye.

No, no, no.

"What are you going to get next?" Daisy asked him.

That was what she always asked Danny! He felt his teeth ground together and his hands fisted at his sides. Danny couldn't take it anymore. "You know what I want next?" Danny asked rather loudly, interrupting their conversation.

The artist and Daisy turned their attention to him.

"Yeah, what do you want, kid?" he asked.

Danny blew out air from his nose and his nostrils flared. *"I want all of your designs."*

Daisy frowned. "Danny–"

The tattoo artist scoffed. "You couldn't afford it, kid. Excuse me for a moment, I got another customer."

But their voices were drowned out by the sudden pain that began knifing into Danny's arm and another on his leg. His skin began to sting and drip with blood. He started to tremble and shake as he stared at Daisy, experiencing the excruciating slicing into skin. Then when one tattoo was completed, he felt another one being cut into another area, this time on his chest.

Daisy's eyes widened as she watched sections of his clothes begin to bloom with red.

"What's happening?" Daisy asked, confused.

Daisy stepped back as blood dripped onto the floor from Danny's shoe.

She shook her head as horror played across her features. "Danny . . . ?"

"Isn't this what you want?" Danny reached out a hand dripping with blood.

Daisy's eyes widened. She turned and ran.

Daisy ran wildly through the crowd. She didn't understand what was happening with Danny. All she knew was that she was completely freaked out! She pushed through a couple of adults and maneuvered around informational tables.

She needed a place to hide. Maybe if she hid, Danny would give up and just go home. She peered over her shoulder, but Danny was still after her!

Her heart beat rapidly in her chest. She found a hallway off to the side. There was a sign that read: NO TRESPASSING, but she didn't care. She needed to get away from Danny.

She ran as fast as she could. She wasn't exactly a good runner and her breaths were gushing out of her mouth. She felt her face flash hot as she tried a couple of doors in the hallway, only to find them locked!

She hit at the doors, frustrated that she couldn't get in.

Danny stumbled down the hallway toward her and she screamed. There was even more blood on him. Some dripped down his face and neck.

What's wrong with him?

"Someone open the door!" she cried. "Please!"

"Daisy, stop!" Danny yelled at her.

She rushed to the next door and twisted the handle to

find it unlocked! She pushed through and rushed inside. She flicked on the light switch and slammed the door closed and locked it. She was in a little office with a desk and a few chairs.

She stepped back, trying to get her breathing under control. She heard Danny stumble closer.

"*Daisy*," he moaned from behind the door. A tear ran down her cheek. She was so scared. She wanted her mom, her dad, and Ms. Gladys.

"Don't run . . . away." He tapped slowly on the wood. *Tap . . . tap . . . tap.* "Please . . . Daisy."

"Just go away, Danny! I mean it!" she shouted at him through the barrier. "I don't want to see you right now!"

"Daisy . . . open the door."

She heard him sniffle and cry.

"I didn't mean . . . for this . . . to happen. I just . . ."

Daisy wiped her own tears and stepped closer to the door to listen since his voice seemed to fade in and out.

". . . liked you . . . so much. I wanted you to feel the same . . ."

Daisy's eyes widened and she stared at the door.

"I tried to get you . . . to notice me . . . with the drawings in your locker."

That had been him? Daisy silently questioned. *He really liked me all this time?*

"Then with the skin designs you liked so much . . ."

Danny didn't say any more.

Still scared, she waited another moment.

"Danny?" She leaned her head against the door. "Are you still there?"

No answer.

What should I do? she wondered. She ran her hands

through her sweaty hair. Maybe Danny needed her help. Maybe she should get him home or to the hospital or something.

Gosh, she never had to worry about someone else before! She liked to act like she knew it all, but she knew she didn't know everything. She was just a kid!

Taking a breath, she braced herself, unlocked the door, and slowly opened it. She looked down at the floor to see a puddle of blood.

She slapped a hand to her mouth to hold back another scream. She leaned forward, looked left and then right down the hall, but there was no sign of Danny.

"Danny?" She looked down at the blood once again and spotted a trail of red leading down the hallway. She took a breath and carefully stepped over the puddle.

Danny was obviously sick. Yeah, she was scared, but he was her friend. She needed to help him. Somehow.

Daisy walked down the hall following the drips of blood and a few bloody footprints. She spotted smeared handprints on the wall leading down another hallway. She found his shoes on the floor spotted with blood. The lights were dim and she couldn't see very clearly.

"Danny, I'm sorry," she called out. "Um, I won't run anymore. I just got a little scared, that's all. Where are you?" She stepped slowly down the walkway. "We should get you home to your mom so you can get help. Okay?"

Her foot kicked something on the ground and she recoiled, uncertain what it could be. When she was certain it wasn't moving, she leaned down closer.

"What is that?" she murmured. It looked a little folded over and was a strange pinkish and off-white color. She rolled it flat with the tip of her tennis shoe.

It was in a shape of daisy.

Daisy blinked, oddly flattered.

There was a funny smell to the flower, and she couldn't figure out what it was made of. She stepped over it and spotted another piece of something strange on the floor. This time it was in the shape of a little heart, and it was also smeared with blood.

Daisy tilted her head as she looked at the texture of the heart and then back at the flower. She shook her head.

It couldn't be . . .

Her pulse started to quicken and her stomach felt funny. She put a hand to her gut and walked forward to the next object on the floor. This one was in the shape of a crescent moon . . .

Hesitantly, she moved forward, not willing to accept what she was seeing and not able to stop herself. There was a little voice in her head that told her: *Turn around! Go back! Run away!* But when she spotted Danny's bloody shirt thrown on the floor, she kept going.

The next bloody shape she found on the ground was of a rocket ship.

Then more . . .

Little cutouts of stars.

A deer.

A hawk.

A tiger.

A guitar.

Music notes.

Smiley faces.

More flowers.

All smeared with blood, and now it seemed like the shapes were turning a darker pink.

No. She kept shaking her head, telling herself what she was actually seeing couldn't be real.

She must be dreaming. It felt like she was living a real-life nightmare.

Suddenly the blood trail widened and there were more of Danny's clothes. Daisy started to tremble.

That is an awful lot of blood. Someone can't lose this much blood unless . . .

More clumps of shapes were on the floor—this time bigger—leading up to the entrance of a dark room. These were more heart shapes, large and oddly maroon and possibly purple. It almost looked like these shapes had been pieced together. That odd smell was so strong, she gagged. Daisy slapped a hand to her nose and mouth so she wouldn't throw up.

She found Danny's cell phone on the floor next. It was smeared with blood and it was vibrating. She didn't pick it up, but she could see on the screen that there were missed calls from his dad and mom.

"Danny?" she whispered this time. She was even more scared than she had been before. She was trembling so badly as she stepped in the doorway. She reached out a shaky hand along the wall to search for a light switch. "Are . . . you . . . there?"

She felt the switch and flicked it on.

There lay a small clump of something in a red puddle.

Hesitantly, Daisy stepped closer, and as realization dawned, she opened her mouth to release a bloodcurdling scream.

The final clump in the center of the room was a silent and still human heart.

ABOUT THE
AUTHORS

Scott Cawthon is the author of the bestselling video game series *Five Nights at Freddy's*, and while he is a game designer by trade, he is first and foremost a storyteller at heart. He is a graduate of the Art Institute of Houston and lives in Texas with his family.

Kelly Parra is the author of YA novels *Graffiti Girl, Invisible Touch*, and other supernatural short stories. In addition to her independent works, Kelly works with Kevin Anderson & Associates on a variety of projects. She resides in Central Coast, California, with her husband and two children.

Andrea Rains Waggener is an author, novelist, ghost-writer, essayist, short story writer, screenwriter, copywriter, editor, poet, and a proud member of Kevin Anderson & Associates' team of writers. In a past she prefers not to remember much, she was a claims adjuster, JCPenney's catalog order-taker (before computers!), appellate court clerk, legal writing instructor, and lawyer. Writing in genres that vary from her chick-lit novel, *Alternate Beauty*, to her dog how-to book, *Dog Parenting*, to her self-help book, *Healthy, Wealthy, & Wise*, to ghostwritten memoirs to ghostwritten YA, horror, mystery, and mainstream fiction projects, Andrea still manages to find time to watch the rain and obsess over her dog and her knitting, art, and music projects. She lives with her husband and said dog on the Washington Coast, and if she isn't at home creating something, she can be found walking on the beach.

Kelly!" Lucia called. "Stop!"

Kelly, who was careening through the dining room—sobbing and stumbling over endoskeleton parts and human limbs—didn't respond. She didn't slow down, either. Not until she tripped over a bar-height chair and fell. She landed full on her front, her arms and legs splayed.

Lucia rushed forward. Kicking aside a crumpled purple paper tablecloth, she dropped to her knees next to Kelly's left hip. "Kelly? Are you okay?" She looked down at Kelly's still form, at her torn, filthy clothes.

Just a few hours before, Kelly's tan crop top and olive capri pants had been pristine. Lucia remembered feeling envious of how good Kelly had looked.

Envy. Now that was a hoot. What a wasted emotion. If Lucia had known then, meandering clueless through the bright, shiny carnival with her friends (and not friends), what was ahead of her, she would never have wasted a single second of her life on envy.

Kelly moaned, rolled over, and sat up. She rubbed a growing knot on her forehead and winced.

Lucia frowned at the reddening lump. "Are you dizzy?" Lucia asked.

Kelly shook her head. "I don't think so." Using the back of her hand, Kelly wiped her eyes and snuffled.

Lucia shifted position and scooted over to sit next to Kelly. *I should be crying, too*, Lucia thought.

Jayce was dead. Sweet, harmless Jayce. Jayce, who Lucia had treated like crap. Jayce, who had kissed Lucia like she'd never been kissed before right before he went off to die.

The kiss had changed everything. It had thrown Lucia's emotions into total chaos, tossing out the window all that she'd thought she knew about boys, about what she'd thought she felt for Adrian and what she'd thought she hadn't felt for Jayce. It turned out that Lucia had liked Jayce a lot more than she'd thought she did. But now it didn't matter. He was gone.

But Lucia didn't have the luxury of trying to sort through the landscape of her heart. She needed her focus for something else entirely. If Jayce's death was to mean anything—he'd given his life to trap the Mimic—and if Lucia and Kelly were going to survive, Lucia needed every bit of her mind to come up with a plan.

Lucia used her shoulder to nudge Kelly. "Now that the Mimic is confined," Lucia said, "we have time to look for a way out."

"We already tried, remember?" Kelly mumbled.

Lucia snorted. "We were running around like a

stampeding herd trapped in a pen," she said. "We neve really tried hard to get through any of the debris block ng the windows and doors. We need to assess the exits pick the one that looks the most accessible, and figure ou how to get through it."

Kelly sniffed and turned to look at Lucia. Lucia stiff ened. Kelly's eyes, though rimmed in red, were dark anc steely. She squinted at Lucia and pressed her lips togethe

She's judging me for not crying, Lucia thought.

"Kelly—" Lucia began.

A loud crack echoed through the building. Kell gasped and started to tremble.

Lucia cocked her head and listened. The building was silent for a full minute. Then Lucia heard a clank. A series of softer clinks followed. And after that, a metallic ending sound reached out from the far end of the hal and scored through the dining room like a physica assault.

"It's the Mimic," Kelly whispered.

Before Lucia could respond, Kelly was on her feet Her eyes wide, her gaze whipping right and left, Kelly's mouth was stretched into a distorted rictus. Kelly whim pered and took off, sprinting toward the archway leading to the pizzeria's lobby.

Here we go again, Lucia thought. Right after Jayce' final scream had ended and Lucia and Kelly had helc each other in their grief, Kelly had lost her mind anc bolted. Now she was doing it again.

Lucia scrambled to her feet. "Kelly, wait!" she shouted

Kelly didn't wait. She kept going; she was back into the full-on panic mode she'd been in before she'd fallen fla on her face. Hurdling over an upturned table and dashing around a pile of lumber, Kelly ran as if the Mimic was right on her heels . . . instead of at the far end of the restaurant trapped in the storage room.

"Kelly!" Lucia tried again.

Lucia trotted after her friend. As she did, she listened to the continuing racket coming from the opposite side of the pizzeria. Yes, it was the Mimic. But it was confined. It could bash and bang all it wanted. It wasn't getting out.

Lucia heard another loud clank.

Her steps faltered.

What if the Mimic *did* get out?

Lucia shook off the thought. She followed Kelly's frenzied progress through the lobby, and she watched when Kelly threw herself at the pile of rubble blocking the pizzeria's main door.

Kelly grunted, struggling to shift a concrete slab. She was panting and making little mewling sounds at the back of her throat. She was also muttering under her breath. "Come on, come on, come on." She whispered the words like they were a mantra that would give her strength.

Lucia reached Kelly's side, and Kelly looked up. She clenched her teeth and gestured at the concrete with her chin.

"Help me move this," she urged.

Lucia shook her head. "Kelly, there's no point."

Kelly shook her head wildly. Her long brown hair, tangled and stringy with sweat, whipped over her cheeks. She stared through the strands, the whites of her eyes nearly bulging from her face. She kept straining to move the concrete slab.

When Lucia didn't make a move to help, Kelly looked up at Lucia and screamed, "Don't just stand there! Help me move this! We have to get out of here!"

A thud resounded in the distance. Lucia felt the muscles in her jaw tighten. She forced herself to relax them. She bent over and put a hand on Kelly's shoulder.

Kelly immediately flung away Lucia's hand. "Don't touch me!" Kelly yelled. "Just help me move this!"

Lucia squatted next to Kelly and tried to grab Kelly's grasping hand. Kelly was clawing at the concrete. Her nails were tearing; blood was running from her fingertips. Still, she wrestled with the heavy slab.

Lucia reached out and grabbed Kelly's wrists. Kelly tried to shake Lucia off. Lucia held on.

The two grappled for several seconds. Kelly finally managed to get one hand free. She reared back and slapped Lucia across the face. One of her broken nails gouged Lucia's cheek.

Lucia didn't think. She just reacted. She slapped Kelly back. Hard. "Stop it!" Lucia screamed.

Kelly continued to thrash. Lucia reached past Kelly's swinging arms and grabbed her shoulders. "Kelly!" she shouted. "Listen to me! Just listen for a second!"

When Kelly kept fighting, Lucia shook her. Kelly finally went limp. Her breath came in long, ragged heaves.

Lucia let go of Kelly and stepped back. "We can't get out this way, Kelly," she said quietly.

Kelly didn't respond.

"Even if we moved all these concrete chunks," Lucia continued, "the door is blocked on the other side by a mountain of poured concrete. Remember? We saw it before we broke in here."

Kelly's head dropped forward. She swayed on her feet but stayed upright. She stared at the floor.

Lucia started to put an arm around Kelly's shoulder, wanting to reassure her that they'd find a way out . . . just not this way. The next sound she heard, though, had her choking on the words she'd been intending to use.

The sound wasn't as loud as the other sounds they'd heard. It was just a clatter and a scrape. But the volume of the sound wasn't the issue. It was its location. The sound wasn't coming from the storage room. It was coming from someplace a little closer than that.

The Mimic was no longer contained.

After the Mimic had dismantled the unit that had been in the little tunnel, it had turned and assessed its surroundings. Its visual and auditory processors had registered one small enclosed room. One door. Seventeen boxes, five opened and twelve unopened. Eighteen toys—eleven plush animals and seven dolls. One of the dolls stared at the Mimic. The Mimic determined that the doll should be handled the way it had learned to handle all endoskeleton-like objects. Such objects had a head, a torso, two arms, and two legs. The Mimic was programmed to break off the limbs and heads.

The Mimic had leaned over, picked up the pig-tailed doll, and ripped its head from its body. It then tore off its arms and legs. Dropping the parts in a pile near one wall of the small room, the Mimic had turned and studied the room's door.

The Mimic knew how to open a door, so it had walked over and grasped the door's handle. It turned the handle, but the door wouldn't open. It exerted more once. Wood cracked, and the handle came free of the door. The Mimic looked at it and tossed the handle onto the pile of doll parts.

The Mimic had then reached into the hole the handle had left behind. It pulled the door open. Now the Mimic faced a solid expanse of metal—a tabletop that blocked the doorway. It had no established protocol for getting through a solid wall, so it turned away from the metal.

The Mimic was not designed to be confined in a room, so it had accessed what it had learned about exiting rooms. It immediately recalled watching the boy unit squirm into the little tunnel, which was the other way out of the room. The Mimic would copy the boy unit and go out of the room that way.

The Mimic had pushed aside a stack of boxes to gain access to the entrance of the small tunnel. It bent over. The tunnel opening was small. Its head fit through the opening, but its shoulders didn't. This wasn't a problem. The Mimic simply needed to take a different form. It was programmed to do this; it could take any form necessary to fulfill its functioning.

So, the Mimic had reconfigured itself and then crawled into the tunnel.

The tunnel was rectangular in shape, and it was made of metal. It slanted upward. The Mimic's metal limbs scraped against the side of the tunnel's metal as it climbed to the top of the narrow enclosure. Its auditory processors registered a long grinding sound as it moved. It had to use the sharp tips of its fingers to pierce the metal so it wouldn't slide backward down the tunnel. Stabbing at the metal to gain purchase, then compressing and contracting its limbs to fit within the confined space, the

Mimic was able to heft itself to the top of the tunnel's slope and launch itself into the next section of the vent.

Lucia didn't hesitate. She grabbed Kelly's hand.

"Come on, Kelly," Lucia urged. "We need to go."

Lucia started to pull Kelly back toward the archway, but Kelly resisted. "Where are you going? We have to get *out*!"

Lucia gritted her teeth and listened to a series of metal-on-metal scratches. The scratches sounded like they were coming from all over the building, as if huge insects were crawling through the walls and the floors. No, not the walls and the floors. The ducts. The Mimic somehow had made it into the ductwork. So much for the idea of it being too heavy for the metal passageways.

Lucia gripped Kelly's hand harder. "I know we need to get out," Lucia said, "but I told you, we can't get out this way. And whichever way we try to get out, it's not going to be fast enough. It won't take the Mimic long to find a vent cover and get out of the ductwork. I have an idea that should buy us some time, but we have to go. Now!"

Kelly blinked, then nodded.

Lucia exhaled in relief. She squeezed Kelly's hand and began leading her back into the dining room.

It didn't matter how many times Lucia crossed through this shamble of broken tables and chairs, chaotic piles of construction material, and mounds of metal and human body parts— Lucia's skin crawled **every time**. The room wasn't so much a room as it was a tomb, a chaotic explosion of death and decay.

Lucia kicked aside a few beleaguered party favors as she aimed for one of the tangled piles of endoskeleton parts. Reaching the mound of metal, she let go of Kelly's hand, bent over, and extracted two endoskeleton arms. She hefted them, studied them, and nodded. "These should work," she said.

Kelly frowned but didn't ask any questions. Her gaze was glassy and unfocused. Lucia was pretty sure Kelly was in shock.

Tucking the endoskeleton arms under her left arm, Lucia took Kelly's hand again. She led Kelly toward the far edge of the stage at the back of the dining room. She heard Kelly's foot kick a paper cup; the cup skittered across the black-and-white floor tiles and spun in a circle at the base of the stage.

"Where are we going?" Kelly asked.

A gut-clenching thrum and thunderous rattle coursed through the pizzeria. These were followed by a sonorous clang.

"I'll tell you in a minute," Lucia said. "We need to hurry. I'm pretty sure the Mimic's out of the duct-work now."

Kelly began breathing faster. Her audible *puff-puff-puffs* kept time with the patter of their footsteps as Lucia led Kelly up onto the stage and back through the heavy red curtain.

Once Lucia let the thick velvet fabric drop behind them, she quickly surveyed the dim backstage area. The small room near the back was the best place, she decided. It had what they needed, and it was close to one of the pizzeria's back exits.

Lucia urged Kelly forward. "This is what we're going to do," Lucia said. She gently pushed Kelly ahead of her into the small room she and the others had found behind the hidden door when they'd gone in search of what they'd thought were other people trapped in the building. It hadn't been people waiting in the little room—it had been the Mimic—and they'd had to run away from the room quickly. Before they had, though, Lucia had seen that the room was filled with costumes.

Lucia heard another clatter. It was closer than the last one. The sheering screeches of metal on metal had stopped. The Mimic was for sure out of the ducts now. Lucia wished she knew where it had come out. Not that it mattered. Wherever it was, Lucia and Kelly didn't have much time.

Lucia set the two endoskeleton arms on the floor, leaning them against the doorjamb. Then she rushed over to a faux fur costume that looked like a blue spotted dog. She eyed it and Kelly; she nodded. Snatching up the costume, she held it out to Kelly.

"You need to get into this costume," Lucia said.

Kelly's face screwed up in disgust. "What? Why?" She backed away from the ragged torn and matted fur.

Lucia didn't blame Kelly for her reaction. The costumes were mildewy and moth-eaten. Who knew what bugs lurked within them? But being bitten by bugs was better than being dismembered.

Lucia held on to the blue dog costume as she scanned the other costumes. She spied a bright court jester costume. The costume was the only one in the room that wasn't made of faux fur, and it looked cleaner than the rest of them. Lucia stepped up to the costume, suppressing a shiver at the jester's leering, toothy grin and its wide eyes. In contrast to the jester's maniacal grin, its colors were cheerful and vivid; its face and its jester hat and tunic were half raspberry-pink and half greenish-yellow. Lucia reached for the silky material, opened up the suit, and started to put her arm inside it.

As soon as Lucia's hand slipped into the jester costume sleeve, she recoiled and snatched her hand back. She stumbled away from the costume, her breath spurting in agitated gasps.

"What is it?" Kelly asked. Her tone was edgy and pitched upward. She was poised to run.

Lucia shook off her alarm and turned away from the court jester. "It's okay. I just almost got into a springlock suit is all."

"A springlock suit?"

Lucia looked around at the other costumes. She started toward a grayish rodent costume—a rat? a mouse? It didn't matter. Lucia grabbed the rodent costume and turned toward Kelly.

"I read about springlock suits in one of the manuals I found in the office," Lucia said. "They have metal clamps that are designed to lock on to the wearer, but their design was faulty. The clamps are lethal. They can literally crush the wearer."

Kelly looked at the other two costumes Lucia held. Her brows bunched together.

"These two are okay," Lucia said.

"I don't get why we need to get in a costume at all," Kelly said.

"We're getting into costumes," Lucia explained, "because I think that once we're in costume, we'll blend into the surroundings here. Obviously, the Mimic, for whatever reason, is following some protocol to dismember humans. It clearly doesn't destroy these characters, though, because they're all intact. If we look like just another Fazbear Entertainment character, it should leave us alone."

Kelly frowned and stared at the costumes. She chewed on her lower lip.

Lucia once again pressed the dog costume toward Kelly. This time, Kelly, with obvious reluctance, took the costume.

Lucia immediately began slipping into the rodent costume. Her lip curled involuntarily. The costume reeked. It wasn't just mildewy. It stank of sweat; it smelled gamey and rancid, like it was the putrefied carcass of an actual rodent as opposed to a costume.

Kelly began struggling to get into the dog costume. "Ew," she complained. "It stinks."

"Yeah," Lucia said. She didn't bother to point out that stink can't kill you, whereas being found by the Mimic definitely would.

The rodent costume was stiff. Lucia had to bunch up her skirt to get her legs into the costume, and the costume's interior abraded her bare legs. She could tell from the crackling sound of Kelly's costume that it was as rigid as Lucia's was. Kelly didn't complain anymore, though. She just wormed her way into the blue dog costume and zipped up the front of its torso. She held the dog's head in her hands. Her face was dirty, pale, tear streaked, and taut. She looked at Lucia.

"Are you sure this is going to work?" Kelly asked.

Lucia zipped herself into the rodent costume. She grasped the big-eared, broken-whiskered head. "It should. But for it to work, we're going to have to be perfectly still when the Mimic is close by."

Lucia canted her head and listened. She didn't hear anything. The pizzeria was silent except for Kelly's continued agitated breathing and the pounding in Lucia's ears. The pounding, she realized, was the beating of her heart. She might have been pretending to be calm, but her body knew how she really felt. The drumming of her rapid-fire heartbeat was like a demented drum circle drubbing a louder and louder beat through her whole body.

Lucia ignored the internal clamor. "Here's what we'll do," she said. She tucked the rodent head under her arm and gestured for Kelly to do the same with the blue dog head. "We're going to see if we can uncover the exit door at the rear of the backstage area. I noticed when we were all trying to get out . ." Lucia stopped. She was suddenly inundated by the reality of what they'd been through. Just a few hours before, all eight of them had been looking for a way out of the building. Now she and Kelly were the only ones left.

Lucia worked her mouth to summon up enough saliva to swallow. She shook off the gag that tried to well up her esophagus. She cleared her throat and tried again. "When we were all trying to get out, I noticed the concrete slabs over the door back here had crumbled more than the slabs over the other windows and doors. They're in smaller chunks. I think we might be able to use these endoskeleton arms to lever the chunks away from the door. Maybe."

Lucia shrugged. What else was there to say? They had to do something. Or just give up and die. Lucia wasn't ready to do that.

Lucia motioned for Kelly to follow her. They stepped

toward the doorway. Lucia picked up the two endo-skeleton arms, and she and Kelly left the small room.

Pausing outside the room, Lucia listened again. Nothing. The Mimic was obviously out of the ductwork, but it wasn't close. She didn't hear the familiar *tap-hiss-rasp* that it made when it walked. She squinted at the gap between the stage curtains. Beyond them, the dining room lights were still glowing. The Mimic wasn't close. Not yet.

"Follow me," Lucia said.

Lucia quickly wove her way through several free-standing racks stuffed with more costumes. Avoiding the open wardrobe where Nick's remains lay, Lucia hurried past a leaning stack of boxes and led Kelly to the backstage exterior door. Its neon EXIT sign was sputtering weakly, providing anemic hope for Lucia's and Kelly's escape.

Putting her back to the potential exit, Lucia looked toward the curtain gap again. The dining room lights still shown through it. The pizzeria was still silent.

Lucia nudged Kelly, who gasped and startled. Then she let out a humorless chuckle. "Sorry," she said.

"Yeah, because you have no reason to be jumpy," Lucia said.

The sarcasm made Kelly chuckle for real. Lucia grinned at her.

"Okay," Lucia said. "We aren't going to be able to work wearing the costume heads, but we need to keep them close."

Lucia bent over and set her rodent head down next to the rubble blocking the door. Kelly followed suit with the blue dog head.

Lucia handed Kelly an endoskeleton arm. "Let's start with these chunks here."

Lucia squatted in front of two of the cracked and deteriorating slabs. She shoved the hand end of the endoskeleton arm between the slabs. Cement dust wafted upward. Lucia's nose twitched; she muffled a sneeze.

Lucia pointed to another clump of concrete. "You work on that one. We'll have to listen, though."

Kelly rolled her eyes. "As if I'd forget to do that," she muttered.

Lucia's lips quirked. There was the Kelly she'd gotten to know over the previous few hours. Maybe Kelly's shock was abating a little.

Lucia stopped prying at the concrete. She listened. She heard nothing. She returned to jimmying the concrete away from the slab next to it. Kelly began poking at a narrow space under her concrete slab.

"Concrete and cement are often used interchangeably," Lucia said softly as she worked. "But actually, cement is just an ingredient in concrete. Concrete is a mix of aggregates—meaning sand and gravel or maybe crushed stone—and paste; the paste is water and cement."

Kelly gave Lucia a *who cares?* look, but Lucia ignored it. Lucia knew Kelly didn't give a darn about the makeup of concrete, but talking about something mundane would help Kelly—and Lucia—keep calm.

"Concrete usually hardens over time, but cracks like these," Lucia gestured at the concrete they were attempting to work free, "can be caused by a number of conditions. Because concrete is porous, it absorbs water. When the water in the concrete freezes, it separates the cement binder from the aggregate and causes crumbling."

"I know," Kelly said. She stopped straining over her block and tilted her head to listen.

Lucia stopped, too. When she heard nothing, she shifted the endoskeleton arm to try to get better leverage. The concrete was shifting a little. Maybe in an hour or so, she'd be able to move one of the slabs away from the door.

Lucia suppressed a sigh. Trying to get out this door was pointless, really. The only reason she was doing it was because she didn't have a better plan . . . yet. Doing nothing, even doing nothing and hiding, was a prescription for a full-on meltdown. And meltdowns weren't conducive to coming up with ideas. Staying busy was essential to keeping it together.

Kelly grunted as she attempted to move her slab again. "Another cause of cracking comes from the aggregate itself," she said. "The minerals in the gravel leech out and start the crumbling."

Lucia raised an eyebrow at Kelly, who glanced over and saw Lucia's expression.

"What?" Kelly said. "I can read, too."

Lucia laughed. Her heart rate slowed; the din in her head quieted a little.

But then Lucia turned and looked toward the slit between the stage curtains. Through the narrow opening, she saw the dining room lights flicker.

"Put the costume head on," Lucia hissed as she set down the endoskeleton arm as quietly as possible. She grabbed the rodent head of her costume.

Kelly didn't hesitate. She copied Lucia's movements instantly.

Together, they donned their costume heads. They both had to speedily tuck their hair up inside the heads. Lucia's frizzy black hair made the costume head a tight fit.

Costume heads in place, Kelly and Lucia straightened

and scurried over to stand in the midst of the other costumes. Then they froze . . . just as the gap between the
stage curtains went black.

The Mimic was close.

Lucia breathed as slowly and evenly through her
mouth as possible, which wasn't that slow. Her heart
rate had ratcheted back into overdrive again. Her body
wanted to pant. It would have been easier to breathe quietly through her nose, but she couldn't do that. The interior
of the rodent head stank even more than the rest of the
costume. The stench was nauseating, so much so that her
stomach had roiled in protest the second she pulled on
the costume head.

Standing just a foot from Lucia, Kelly was clearly
struggling to be quiet, too. She was doing pretty well,
though. Lucia could only hear infinitesimal inhales every
second or so.

Lucia couldn't see Kelly. They were standing side by
side, and Lucia couldn't risk turning her head even a
tiny bit.

Just beyond the stage curtains, the *tap-hiss-rasp* started
coming their way. Through the mesh of the rodent's eye-
holes, Lucia saw the stage curtain flutter. Then it swayed.

And the backstage lights went out.

Total blackness.

Robbed of her vision, Lucia's other senses were turbo-
charged. The pungent odor inside the rodent head got
stronger. The surface of the suit's fabric got rougher.
The Mimic's approaching footsteps got louder. Every tap
ricocheted around the inside of Lucia's head. Every hiss
was drawn out like the angry warning of a snake about
to strike. Every rasp felt like it was excoriating Lucia's

inner ears. Behind the sound of the Mimic's approach, Lucia's breathing and that of Kelly's next to her sounded like deafening wind gusts. Surely, the Mimic would hear them.

Even so, they had to stay still. Running at this point would mean death.

Lucia was tempted to count the passing seconds, but she refrained. She didn't have to mark the time to know it was passing. Her muscles, protesting her statue-like position, were doing a fine job of letting her know how long she and Kelly had been frozen in place. Lucia's knees were beginning to quaver. Her lower back started to ache. The balls of her feet began to burn.

Forcing herself to ignore the sounds of the Mimic's footsteps, Lucia put all her attention on relaxing her muscles as much as possible. Then she began doing math equations in her head. That was a trick her dad had taught her when she was little. When Lucia couldn't get to sleep at night, Lucia's mom had told her to think of something nice. *Imagine being on a picnic or going to the beach,* Lucia's mom had said. Lucia had tried that; it didn't work. Whenever she thought about anything, her mind would take off. One thought was the first domino in a succession of thought dominos. The beach would lead to the sea, which led to boats, which led to fishing, which led to dolphins, which led to dolphins getting caught in nets, etc., and then Lucia would be even more wide-awake. Her dad told Lucia that the problem was the emotions connected to the thoughts. *The trick is math equations, he said. Math is emotionless. Just play with the numbers. It will calm your mind.*

So, now, Lucia played with numbers . . . for a very long time.

Somewhere in the middle of her twelfth complex equation, though, Lucia noticed she wasn't hearing anything. She returned her attention to her senses . . . and she realized the lights were back on.

It had worked! The Mimic was gone.

Just in case, though, Lucia counted to sixty before she moved. At sixty, the lights were still on. The backstage area—no, the entire pizzeria—was silent.

Lucia turned her head slowly to look at Kelly. She could see Kelly's wide eyes staring back at her through the mesh of the blue dog's costume eyes.

Lucia turned again to look around. Everything was the same as it had been before . . . or at least she thought it was. The backstage area was such a jumble of boxes and costumes that it was hard to remember what was where. But it looked okay to Lucia.

She started to raise a hand to remove the rodent head. Thankfully, she'd only raised her hand an inch or so before she saw it.

She froze. And she stared hard at the costumes near the wardrobe.

Lucia had never looked too closely at the costumes in the wardrobe area . . . because of Nick. But she had registered the colors of the costumes without even realizing that she had. She'd seen black, brown, blonde, dirty white, yellow, and pink. Now, however, she was seeing a brighter pink, an almost reddish pink. *Cerise*, Lucia thought inanely.

She would have noticed a cerise costume if it had been there before, especially since the pinkish color was part of a creepy mushroom cap. The cerise and white-spotted mushroom cap was atop a gaping-eyed mushroom "stem" wearing overalls that matched the cerise cap. The mushroom character's face had an eerie, yawning black hole of a mouth. Lucia surely would have noticed the costume if it had been there before.

Lucia caught her breath and held it. She tried to talk herself out of what she was seeing, but she couldn't do it. There was definitely a new costume by the wardrobe. And there could be only one reason for that.

Lucia didn't dare move or make a sound to warn Kelly. All she could do was will Kelly to remain still and hope Kelly was taking Lucia's cue. She hoped Kelly had gotten to know Lucia well enough to reason that if Lucia wasn't moving, she had a reason for staying still.

A full minute passed.

And another.

Kelly did indeed remain frozen. She didn't make a sound . . . until the creepy mushroom moved.

When the mushroom's head turned, Lucia heard Kelly gasp. Every muscle in Lucia's body contracted. She held her breath.

The gasp had been a quiet one. Hopefully the Mimic hadn't heard it.

Lucia stared at the mushroom. Was it going to come this way?

The mushroom rotated; its dark, round eyes inspected the whole backstage area. When the mushroom's gaze fell on Lucia, she closed her own eyes.

A couple seconds later, Lucia opened her eyes, just in time to see the stage lights start to flicker. The mushroom was now walking toward them.

The lights went out.

A half second later, the lights came back on. They came back on just in time for Lucia to see something crawling out of the back of the mushroom costume.

It took all Lucia's willpower not to scream at the top of her lungs. She couldn't believe what she was seeing.

When Hope, just minutes before she had died, described the Mimic, she'd described it as a big, shiny, black metal skeleton. Before Lucia had found the user's manual that told her the thing that had killed Hope was a robot called a Mimic, she and the others had thought of the thing as a creature, but it had been an upright, vaguely man-shaped creature. The drawings Lucia had seen in the manual had depicted an upright creature as well.

The user's manual, however, had said the Mimic could take many forms. Apparently, this was one of its forms.

Creeping out of the back of the overalls-clad mushroom was an abomination of twisted and contorted metal. The abomination was a mass of metal joints and wires that were shaped into something vaguely resembling a mutated spider—with one of its eyes on one leg, and the other on its back. The frightening spider had nine legs instead of a spider's usual eight—one of the legs extended from where its mouth should have been. That leg pulsed through the air like a proboscis seeking something to suck into the scuttling creature's bowels.

Unlike the Mimic's footfalls when it was upright, this configuration of the Mimic's parts made a *tsk-tsk* sound, a sloppy ticking that was at the same time squelching wet and dryly brittle. The sound was much, much worse than the *tap-hiss-rasp*. The sound made every hair on Lucia's body stand on end. It nearly drove her instantaneously mad.

Kelly must have felt the same way. She suddenly made a run for it.

Lucia opened her mouth to shout, "No!" but self-preservation stopped the word from coming out. The thing scooting across the floor might have looked like an alien insect, but it was the Mimic, and the Mimic could hear. If Lucia shouted, she'd give herself away. She didn't move a muscle.

But then Lucia's concern for Kelly overrode thoughts of Lucia's own safety. She couldn't help herself.

"Kelly, stop!" Lucia screamed.

Lucia immediately sucked in her breath. She'd given herself away!

But it was worth it. Kelly stopped. Halfway to the stage curtain, she froze, turning into a furry blue dog statue.

Lucia, staring hard at Kelly, could see the blue dog's tail quiver a little. But otherwise, it was motionless.

Way to go, Kelly, Lucia thought.

Lucia, moving her eyes only, followed the Mimic's progress as it squirmed across the wood floor. Its metal appendages continued to make that *tsk-tsk*. The floor vibrated under the Mimic's weight.

For a second, Lucia thought the Mimic was coming for her. It was moving directly toward her.

But the Mimic didn't approach the stock-still rodent. It kept going on past. It scrabbled over toward the blue dog costume. Lucia stiffened.

The Mimic circled the blue dog. Its proboscis-like extension searched the air around the blue dog costume as if trying to sniff out the costume's authenticity. Twice the Mimic backed away from the blue dog. Each time scooted forward again. It used one appendage to tentatively tap the blue dog's foot.

Don't move, Kelly, Lucia thought.

Somehow, Kelly was holding it together. She didn't move. The Mimic was acting like it was studying the blue dog, as if it was confused by it. Lucia understood the Mimic's reaction. It probably was registering the fact that the dog hadn't been there when the Mimic had first come backstage.

How did the Mimic reason? Lucia wondered. *Would it figure out the ruse?*

The Mimic backed away from the blue dog costume again. It turned and started *tsk-tsk*ing toward the stage curtain.

A near-silent sigh of relief escaped from between Lucia's lips. It was going to be okay.

But then it wasn't.

Suddenly, the Mimic turned again. It skirred back toward the blue dog.

What happened next happened so fast that Lucia's brain was barely able to process it. And she didn't want to process it.

In a nanosecond, one of the Mimic's spidery legs reached out and peeled open the back of the blue dog costume. The instant the costume was breached, the Mimic wormed its way past the edges of the matted blue fur. Inconceivably, shockingly, the Mimic shoved itself *inside* the costume . . . with Kelly.

Lucia heard a sickening crunch.

Kelly, Lucia thought.

She hadn't even finished thinking Kelly's name before Kelly screamed.

The scream speared through Lucia like a lance. It plunged so deeply into Lucia's heart that the pain felt like real, physical pain. Red hot, piercing.

But the scream wasn't the worst of it. The crunch was followed by a snap. Then another.

Kelly's screams went an octave higher. The snapping was joined by splintering sounds—spongy, wet splintering sounds.

The costume's blue fur started going dark. The darkness began at the costume's center mass, and it spread outward quickly. Too quickly.

Lucia heard another crunch.

Kelly stopped screaming.

Lucia wanted to close her eyes and pretend to be someplace else, but that didn't feel right. She couldn't do anything for Kelly now except be a silent witness to Kelly's death. So, Lucia didn't close her eyes. She watched as lumps and bulges writhed under the blood-saturated blue fur. She watched until the blue dog costume began to collapse, folding in on itself, crumpling toward the stage. She continued to watch when the lumpy pile of bloody fur convulsed and then went still.

And she watched when the blood-soaked blue dog costume once again took form, unfolding itself from the stage to stand upright. She continued to watch as the blue dog walked off to the right, out of Lucia's line of sight. When the Mimic was no longer in view, Lucia couldn't bring herself to look away from the blood pool spreading ever wider on the wooden floorboards.